HEAT WAVE

Heat Wave

LEFT BEHIND
>THE KIDS<

Jerry B. Jenkins
Tim LaHaye

WITH CHRIS FABRY

TYNDALE HOUSE PUBLISHERS, INC.
WHEATON, ILLINOIS

Edited by Lorie Popp

ISBN 0-8423-8347-6, mass paper

Printed in the United States of America

08   07   06   05   04
8   7   6   5   4   3   2

To Andrew David Borden

TABLE OF CONTENTS

THE YOUNG TRIBULATION FORCE

Original members—Vicki Byrne, Judd Thompson, Lionel Washington

Other members—Mark, Conrad, Darrion, Janie, Charlie, Shelly, Melinda

OTHER BELIEVERS

Chang Wong—Chinese teenager working in New Babylon

Tsion Ben-Judah—Jewish scholar who writes about prophecy

Colin and Becky Dial—Wisconsin couple

Sam Goldberg—Jewish teenager, Lionel's good friend

Mr. Mitchell Stein—Jewish friend of the Young Trib Force

Naomi Tiberius—computer whiz living in Petra

Chaim Rosenzweig—famous Israeli scientist

Tanya Spivey—daughter of Mountain Militia leader, Cyrus Spivey

Cheryl Tifanne—young lady from Iowa

Zeke Zuckermandel—disguise specialist for the Tribulation Force

Marshall Jameson—leader of the Avery, Wisconsin, believers

UNBELIEVERS

Nicolae Carpathia—leader of the Global Community

Leon Fortunato—Carpathia's right-hand man

What's Gone On Before

JUDD Thompson Jr. and the rest of the Young Tribulation Force are living the adventure of a lifetime. As Lionel and Judd try to get back to their friends in Wisconsin, Lionel's arm is trapped beneath a huge boulder, and Judd rushes for medical help. Lionel realizes his only option is to amputate his arm.

Vicki Byrne and the others at the Avery, Wisconsin, hideout help Cheryl when she goes into labor. After a few stressful hours, Cheryl gives birth to a healthy boy, Ryan Victor. As promised, Cheryl agrees to let Tom and Josey Fogarty care for the child.

Over the next few months, Judd and Lionel stay with a new group of believers in Ohio. Vicki and Judd talk as much as possible, but with all the GC activity, it isn't safe to travel.

Vicki despairs over a change in Cheryl's behavior. The girl has become hostile, and the Fogartys are afraid she might do something to Ryan.

In New Babylon, Chang Wong notices strange reports about a worldwide heat wave. He watches as the fire burns office workers.

Join the Young Tribulation Force as they live out their faith in the most chaotic period of world history.

ONE

The Fourth Bowl

JUDD Thompson Jr. pressed the phone to his ear and walked to a private place in the Ohio hideout. Chang had called from New Babylon to tell Judd about something weird, what he called the "fourth Bowl Judgment." Chang seemed excited about what this might mean for believers.

"Has Dr. Ben-Judah said anything about this?" Judd said.

"I haven't heard anything, but you know he'll come out with something soon."

Judd flipped on the television as he talked, but the only local station was off the air. "Back up and tell me exactly what happened."

Chang took a breath. "I had been listening to Carpathia when his secretary said there were strange reports about a heat wave. Then

1

I heard shouts near my office. Everyone ran to the front window, and my boss warned them to get back. That's when the glass exploded and Rasha . . ." Chang stopped for a moment.

"Who's Rasha?"

"She worked near me. We had several conversations about Judah-ites and all the miraculous things going on. She was a Carpathia follower, but she was really scared that something bad was going to happen to her. I wanted to tell her the truth so many times, but there was no way. She had Carpathia's mark."

"What happened to her?"

"She was at the window when it shattered. Shards of glass flew everywhere. Rasha and another man were cut and fell to the floor as the hot air blew into the room. People went crazy, screaming and running over each other. One woman tried to help Rasha, but her hair burst into flames."

"If that was going on inside, I can't imagine what happened outside."

"It was awful," Chang said. "A woman was walking her dog below us. She let go of the animal and tried to get inside a car, but she burned her hands on the door handles. The dog ran in a circle, trying to find some shade or relief from the heat, but it finally turned into a dog torch."

Judd shuddered. "And the same thing happened to people?"

"They fell out of their cars. Tires exploded. I saw windshields melt. My boss ordered everyone into the basement."

"Could you feel the heat?"

"It was a bit warmer, but I wasn't burned. I pretended it was hurting though."

"What happened to Rasha and the other guy?"

"They turned into human fire. It was awful. The others ran for the elevator, but I said I would catch the next one. I wanted to run to my quarters and alert the Tribulation Force and you."

As soon as he was off the phone, Judd logged on to Tsion Ben-Judah's Web site. Judd couldn't imagine what the last five years would have been like without the spiritual direction of this man. His Web site alone had helped millions come to know God, and the 144,000 evangelists God had raised up had reached more. Judd noticed a new posting from Tsion and downloaded the file so Lionel and the others could read it. Tsion wrote:

> *My dear friends in Christ, I want you to know that we have reached another terrible*

milestone. For those of you in the former
USA and other places where the sun is yet
to rise, the deadly fourth Bowl Judgment
has struck, as prophesied in the Bible, and
every time zone in the world will be
affected.

Here in Petra, by ten in the morning,
people out in the sun without the seal of
God were burned alive. This may seem an
unparalleled opportunity to plead once
again for the souls of men and women,
because millions will lose loved ones. But
the Scriptures also indicate that this may
come so late in the hearts of the undecided
that they will have already been hardened.

Burned alive. Judd couldn't imagine such
horror. He had seen scary movies where
people had been burned, and the images had
stuck in his mind.

Tsion included the Scripture that
mentioned the judgment:

Revelation 16:8-9 says, "Then the fourth
angel poured out his bowl on the sun, and
power was given to him to scorch men with
fire. And men were scorched with great
heat, and they blasphemed the name of God
who has power over these plagues; and they
did not repent and give Him glory."

Tsion's message continued, explaining as much as he could, but the man admitted he did not know how long the heat would last. Judd read the brief message again. He had so many questions. Was Chang right about being able to move around during daylight? If cars had exploded in New Babylon, would the Humvee they had hidden near the hideout also explode, or would God somehow spare believers' vehicles?

Judd wished he could talk with Tsion himself, but he knew that wasn't possible. He recalled a conversation with Rayford Steele, who gave his secure phone number and offered to help in making decisions. Judd glanced at his watch. Before he called Vicki with the news, he had to talk with Captain Steele.

Vicki Byrne hadn't slept well the past few nights. Cheryl's moods swung like playground equipment, but the truth was, the situation with the Fogartys had eased a little. Cheryl had said she didn't need to see Ryan much anymore, and Marshall and Zeke were trying to find her another place to live.

But Vicki had to admit that Cheryl wasn't the only reason she was losing sleep.

Members of the Young Tribulation Force had grown frustrated. Some wanted to take more chances to find people without the mark of Carpathia. Mark had talked about leaving the group and traveling, but Zeke had convinced him to stay.

The newest members of the group, Ty and Tanya Spivey, along with the others who had broken away from Tanya's father's group, had thought the camp in Wisconsin was the next best thing to heaven when they arrived. Now they felt disappointed at the conflict.

"I know we're all human," Tanya had said to Vicki when they were alone one morning, "but the stuff with Cheryl and the fighting between Conrad and Shelly upset me."

"I'm just as disappointed as you," Vicki said, "but when we become believers we're not promised that everything's going to be easy. In a lot of ways, things got worse when I became a believer."

"That doesn't seem fair. If God loves us, wouldn't he help us solve our problems?"

Vicki couldn't think of a Bible passage that addressed the subject, and she had to admit she felt the same way. She wanted God to fix things. The world's troubles had united the kids for a time, but each day brought new struggles.

Something moved outside the cabin, and

Vicki sat up. The moon shone through the curtains, casting an eerie glow. She strained to hear, but all was quiet.

Vicki closed her eyes and prayed for her friends, especially Judd. If God would bring him back, she could put up with any problem.

Judd dialed the number to the hideout in San Diego and took a deep breath.

"Steele," Rayford answered.

"I hope I'm not bothering you, Captain. This is Judd Thompson."

"Not a problem. What's up?"

Judd explained what Chang Wong had told him, and Rayford said he had just gotten off the phone with Dr. Ben-Judah. "I wanted to ask him if those with the seal of God would be immune to the heat."

"My question exactly," Judd said. "What did Tsion say?"

"He said they feel some extra warmth there in Petra and some people are a little tired, but like Chang, they're not feeling the effects like unbelievers."

"Then it's true. I could go out tomorrow morning without the GC knowing about it."

"It's likely. I told Tsion this could mean

a lot to the Trib Force. As long as we hide before GC officers come out, we're okay."

"Which means you can move supplies around the country."

"Exactly. And with the way the groups are begging for food, this comes at a great time."

"I'm trying to get to the Wisconsin hide-out. Do you think it would be safe to drive there tomorrow?"

"You're talking about Avery, right?"

"Yes."

"And what's your location now?"

Judd told him.

"I don't know if I'd chance it unless you have some place to ditch for the night. Wait and see what happens tomorrow. I'll be talk-ing with our people about flights to various groups. Maybe you could tag along."

"Great. But will planes be able to fly in the heat?"

"I hope so. You have to understand we have no idea how long this will last. It could be a few hours, a few days, or weeks. Tsion cautioned that God has never been predict-able with these plagues. We know the order they come in, and we used to think that when one ended the next one began. Now we know they can overlap. Tsion just doesn't want to see us caught in the open when the thing ends."

"Me either. But you know the Global Community has to look at something like this as another nail in their coffin."

"The world's in bad shape. People are scrounging for food and the bare necessities. There's no law except survival. Everybody who's smart goes out with a gun."

"Sort of like the Old West."

"Right, except the good guys are the evangelists. Yesterday I got a report about two who preached to a small town in Germany. There were still a few holdouts to Carpathia's mark, and these evangelists found them, but before they could finish speaking, a group of armed men broke into the meeting. They took all the valuables and Nicks the people had and then separated the men from the women."

"I don't like the sound of this."

"Neither did I, until I heard what happened next. It was clear this gang of thieves was up to no good. But as they were leading the women outside, an angel appeared at the door, and with a couple of words the robbers all fell dead."

"What happened to the others?"

"All of them believed the message and received the mark of God."

Judd shook his head. "I'd almost given up

about any undecided. It seems like everybody's chosen Carpathia or God."

"This is the greatest rescue mission the
earth has ever known. On the video reports
about the wrath of the Lamb earthquake,
people dug through collapsed buildings for
days, even weeks, looking for just one survivor. In one hospital, they found a baby alive
fifteen days after the earthquake. I like to
think our mission is the same. We have to
keep digging, keep praying, keep hoping that
we'll find someone who's ready to hear the
message."

"I hadn't thought about it that way," Judd
said.

"People have lost faith in the GC and its
leaders. If there's anyone out there without
Carpathia's mark, and we can get to them,
I have to believe they'll choose the light
instead of darkness.They're going to be
suffering as the sun rises every day."

Judd paused. "But hasn't Dr. Ben-Judah
said God is actually showing mercy with
these judgments?"

"I asked him about that, and he still thinks
the fact that more plagues are coming means
God still wants people to repent. Most won't
and will curse God, but Tsion supports our
efforts to find the remaining undecided."

"Then I want to be part of it. And I'll bet

there's a bunch of people in Wisconsin who would too and some here in Ohio."

"Let's see what the morning brings," Rayford said. "In the meantime, call Vicki and tell her the good news."

"You know about us?"

"Chloe told me. My guess is you two will be back together within a couple of days."

Judd couldn't help but smile as he hung up. He had tried to stay reserved with Captain Steele, but he was sure some of his excitement had come through on the phone. He quickly dialed Vicki's number.

Vicki awoke with a start. She couldn't tell how long she had been sleeping. Was it an hour? two? The moon had moved little in the window, so she guessed she hadn't been asleep long.

Something outside had startled her. Or had it been a dream? It sounded like Marshall's van, but who could be taking it this time of night?

For the first time in a long while, Vicki worried about the Global Community. What if they had discovered the remote camp? She wrapped a blanket around her shoulders, grabbed a flashlight, and tiptoed outside.

The ground was wet with dew, and the crisp temperature raised goose bumps on her arms. She headed for the main cabin where the others usually gathered and saw footsteps heading toward Josey and Tom Fogarty's cabin. When she pointed the flashlight at their front door, she noticed it was open a few inches.

Someone stirred inside, and a light came on.

"Mrs. Fogarty?" Vicki whispered.

A shriek pierced the night.

Vicki rushed toward the cabin as Tom Fogarty swung the door open. "Where is he?"

"Where's who?" Vicki said.

Josey bounded to the door behind him. "He's gone! Ryan's gone!"

TWO

Missing

VICKI rushed inside the cabin and saw Ryan's empty bed. On Ryan's second birthday, Zeke had given the boy a toddler bed in the shape of a car. The child's blanket was gone and a stuffed bear lay on the floor.

Tom Fogarty had run out the door as soon as Vicki arrived. Josey shook while she ran around the room, looking under the bed, checking in the closet. "Sometimes he'll play hide-and-seek and I won't find him until he laughs, but he's never run off at night. Ryan started sleeping at night, you know."

Vicki took Josey's arm and gently pulled her onto the bed. "Tell me what happened."

"We just woke up and he was gone! It's so chilly outside, and the little thing didn't have shoes on."

"I saw footprints outside, but they didn't look like a child's."

13

Tom Fogarty ran inside breathing hard, his face pale. Marshall followed him in.

"Did you find him?" Josey said.

"We checked Cheryl's cabin," Tom said. "She's not there."

"Look in the other cabins," Josey said. "Check the meeting place or—"

Marshall held up a hand. "Ma'am, the van's gone. I usually keep the keys hidden, but somehow she must have found them."

"You think Cheryl . . . ?" Josey's voice trailed off, and her eyes fluttered. Suddenly she locked eyes with Tom. "Then we have to go after him. We have another car—"

"Hang on," Marshall said. "We're going after her and Ryan. Zeke and Mark have gone for the car. She's gotten a head start, but hopefully she hasn't gone far."

While Tom tried to calm Josey, Vicki followed Marshall outside. "Let me go with you. When we catch up to her I can—"

"We've already decided you need to go," Marshall said. "Get dressed and meet us at the car."

When Judd didn't get an answer in Wisconsin, he e-mailed Vicki and told her the latest news. Then he checked on the latest from the Global Community.

At first, the GC posted all the grisly pictures. Traffic cameras set up near busy intersections showed melting car tires and people jumping from their vehicles. The people just as quickly tried to get back inside, but the door handles were so hot they couldn't touch them. Frantic, drivers rushed for shade or nearby buildings. Shots from these cameras didn't last long because the cameras themselves went blank after a few seconds.

Reporters standing on rooftops showed the slow-moving arc of the sun as it came over the horizon. When the rays reached houses, they began smoking and smoldering. As the sun rose higher, homes caught fire.

Reporters ran for their lives inside buildings, which eventually collapsed from the heat. Judd found one camera shot from a famous university. The view was shielded by trees and looked out on a fountain in the middle of the campus. As the sun beat down, water bubbled. Soon it was boiling and steam rose.

On a gentle slope nearby, a student lay in the shade holding a book, his head propped up on a backpack. He sat up when the water boiled. Suddenly, as trees caught fire and smoke rose, the boy grabbed his backpack and stood.

"Get out of there," Judd whispered to himself.

The boy ran but made the mistake of rushing toward the sunlight. Like a vampire caught in daylight, the boy turned, shielded his face from the hot rays, and fell. First his backpack, then the boy's clothes caught on fire. Finally, he became part of the burning landscape, with trees, bushes, and even the grass igniting.

Judd clicked to one of his favorite sites, which showed famous beaches. The only cameras operating were those where the sun hadn't yet risen, but reports stated the blood was boiling in oceans around the globe.

Everywhere the sun reached, people, animals, plant life, buildings, cars, bridges, and homes were affected. The world had become the wick of a candle that was quickly burning up, and Judd wondered how many could survive another year before the Glorious Appearing of Jesus Christ.

Judd wrote his friend Sam Goldberg and asked for a report from Petra. He wanted to know exactly what to expect when the sun came up over Ohio.

Vicki rushed to her cabin and dressed, then met Tom, Marshall, and Mark. It took a few minutes for them to back the small four-wheel-drive vehicle from its hiding place. As different people had traveled to the hideout to see Zeke or join the group, one problem Marshall and the others had to deal with was the extra vehicles left in the woods nearby. The group decided to keep the van handy and hide the others. A few cars had been driven into the Mississippi River.

Vicki and Mark climbed in the back, Marshall driving and Tom Fogarty beside him. Vicki thought Tom was perfect for the trip since he had been a former police officer, but she wondered how he had convinced Josey to stay behind.

"Cheryl's obviously been planning this for some time," Tom said. "Vicki, you've talked the most with her. Has she ever said anything about leaving?"

Vicki shook her head. "These past few weeks we haven't talked about much at all. She's been so grouchy that I've had to leave her alone."

The car bounced along the rutted dirt road. When they reached a paved road, Tom got out and inspected the area. "Go left," he said.

Mark reached for the phone and dialed the hideout. He turned on the speakerphone and asked Conrad to search the computer for anything Cheryl might have written.

"Be right back to you," Conrad said.

"I can't imagine what that little guy's going through right now," Tom said. "Hopefully he'll sleep through this whole thing until we catch them."

Conrad called a few moments later. "I found a deleted message from Wanda, the midwife who helped deliver Cheryl's baby."

"What's it say?" Mark said.

"She was actually writing to Mrs. Fogarty."

"What?" Tom said. "Josey hasn't had any contact with her in months."

"Let me read you the letter," Conrad said.

> "Dear Josey,
>
> "I'm sorry to hear things have gone so badly with little Ryan. Babies can be a handful, especially if he has an illness like you described. If there's anything I can do from this end to help, please let me know. Otherwise, your plan to send Cheryl here with him sounds good. I'd be glad to keep them with me until they can make other arrangements. Be advised that I'm in a different location. I'll include a map on this e-mail, and you can let me know what you want to do. There's plenty of room to park the van, so don't worry about that, but be careful of the GC as you hit town.
>
> "No matter what happens, know that I'll

be praying for you and your husband and Ryan through this difficult time. Remember, we serve a great God who can indeed work miracles."

Vicki ran a hand through her hair. "Cheryl wrote to Wanda pretending to be your wife and lied about Ryan being sick!"

Tom shifted in his seat and pursed his lips. "Conrad, are there any other deleted messages there?"

"I'm checking." *Click. Click.* "Okay, found two. The first one looks like . . . yeah, this is the one where she describes Ryan as having an illness and that she wants permission for Cheryl to take Ryan to Wanda's house."

Marshall rolled to a stop at a major road and turned off the headlights. "I'm assuming Wanda is in the same general area where we found her last time?"

"Yeah, I'll give directions in a minute," Conrad said. "Just head toward her old place."

"What's the next message say?" Tom said. *Click.* "Oh, boy . . . here we go."

"Dear Wanda,
"Thanks for your kindness and prayers. The situation with Ryan has gotten even worse since I last wrote. Would it be possi-

ble, if we can work it out with Marshall and the others, to have Cheryl come alone with Ryan and stay at your place? We would send her in the van.

"I agree with you that God can work miracles. I would like nothing better than to have Ryan back, but all the crying and sleepless nights have Tom and me at the end of our rope. Cheryl has been so good to help us. I don't know what we'd have done without her. We're all praying that God will heal Ryan on the way to your place. You pray with us and we'll look for a good report once Cheryl is there."

"She signs the letter, *'Yours in Christ, Josey.'* "

Tom slammed his fist so hard on the glove compartment that Vicki thought he had broken his hand. Marshall drove as fast as he dared, using the moonlight to navigate. Conrad read the directions to Wanda's house, and Mark took notes.

"Vicki, you have a new message here from Judd," Conrad said. "And it looks like I've missed a couple of his calls."

Vicki smiled. "I'll read it when I get back."

"Hang on. Zeke has something to say to you guys," Conrad said.

"How's my wife doing?" Tom said.

"As well as can be expected," Zeke said. "She tore out of the cabin when you left. Took three of us to get her back to her room and settled down. Shelly and Darrion are with her, and I've got Charlie standing watch to make sure nobody bothers her."

"What did you want, Zeke?" Marshall said.

"Well, you know I'm not into bad feelings and that kinda stuff, but I gotta tell you I'm worried about you guys and little Ryan."

"We're going to catch her, believe me," Tom said.

"I know, but there are GC in that area. I just looked at their list of arrests in the past two weeks, and they've made a bunch of surprise raids. Cheryl could be leading you guys right to the enemy."

"Thanks for the heads up," Mark said, "but I don't think we're going to stop until we find Ryan."

Judd heard a blip and noticed Sam was sending a video message from Petra. Judd turned on the small camera above the screen and saw his friend. Sam wanted to know how Lionel was doing.

"He's adjusted pretty well, but he still has some pain," Judd said. "If we can ever get to

Wisconsin, there's a guy who's been working on some kind of contraption he thinks Lionel will be able to use."

"I suppose you've heard what's going on here if you've written at this hour," Sam said.

"Tell me about it," Judd said.

Sam was inside the communications building, but he had someone open the door behind him and Judd could see rock formations in the background. Sam wiped sweat from his forehead. "It's crazy. Some of us noticed it was getting a little warmer, but we had no idea there was a plague until about ten this morning. We heard screams and rushed to see what it was.

"There were some stragglers just outside the camp, undecideds who didn't see the miracle worker. They were literally burned alive where they stood. That's when the reports began coming in from all over the world. We heard from China that everything is dried up, burned, or melted. No one is on the street, except for believers. Some GC apparently tried to use fireproof suits and boots and helmets, but they didn't get very far. One of our sources says believers found piles of burning material on the street."

"So it's kind of like the locusts—the believers can move around without fear they're going to be burned. But one thing still bugs me."

"What's that?"

"If all these buildings are falling in and cars are exploding because of the heat, how do the believers get around? If they walk, they won't get very far. But if they try to use a car or a plane, won't they burn?"

"I don't know how God's doing it, but it seems like the vehicles believers use are immune to the heat. Just like the clothes we wear and our shoes. The same with the hide-outs of believers and the supplies."

"Amazing."

"Dr. Ben-Judah just called for prayer that God would give wisdom to the Tribulation Force about how to use this opportunity."

"Great. But you don't feel anything more than just being a little bit warm?"

"Wait a few hours. You'll feel what it's like soon enough."

Judd closed his eyes and smiled. For the first time in months, things would be reversed. Now the GC would hide during the day and be out at night, and the Young Trib Force would move around during the day and sleep at night.

THREE

The Search

VICKI suggested they call Wanda and warn her about Cheryl, but Marshall reminded her that Wanda didn't use a phone. Marshall asked Conrad to send an urgent e-mail to Wanda detailing what they knew.

As they bounced over back roads, Vicki thought about all they had been through in the past few years. The disappearance of her family would have been enough change, but with the earthquake, the plagues, and Nicolae Carpathia hunting down and killing believers, Vicki had little time to think about the past. Survival was a full-time job, and reaching out to those who didn't know God was her main mission.

Still, hardly a day went by that she didn't think of her family, her friends who had died, and the way things could have been.

Vicki's nineteenth birthday had come and
gone without anyone remembering. Not
even Judd. She didn't blame anyone, but she
still ached for things to return to normal.
Before the disappearances, she had dreamed
of going away to school. She thought a
college degree might help her get a good job,
and who knew, maybe she would find some
rich guy and settle down in a Chicago suburb
in a real house instead of a trailer. But her
parents didn't have the money to send her,
and Vicki wasn't scholarship material, at least
back then.

Vicki wasn't proud of the way she had
lived before the disappearances. She had
made bad choices in friends and in the way
she lived. She had put partying above everything, and she knew she had to tell Judd
about some of those things. Maybe he had
skeletons too.

Before the vanishings, Vicki hadn't thought
of her life in the long term. If something
sounded fun, she did it. If she thought something would make her happy, she'd try it. If
someone suggested a tattoo or a piercing, she
only thought of what people would say the
next day at school.

The vanishings and Vicki's new belief in
God had changed all that. Suddenly, the
truth about Jesus and what he had done for

her, the reality that God wanted her to dedicate her life to him, and the fact that there were only seven years until the return of Jesus made her want to change. God himself transformed the hopes and dreams of a normal teenager.

Vicki could never have dreamed what God would do in those first few years. She recalled a quote that summed up her feelings: "The world has not yet seen what God can do with one person who is totally committed to him." As Vicki became more aware of God, his power and love and how much he wanted to help Vicki, she had grown more confident. In spite of her weaknesses, God was using Vicki.

She mulled these things over as they drove into the night, knowing the others at the hideout would be praying. She wondered about Judd's e-mail and felt sad she hadn't asked Conrad to read it to her. It couldn't be anything embarrassing because Judd and Vicki had agreed they wouldn't use e-mails to talk about things that were too personal. When they were on the phone, they discussed their feelings, but in e-mails they stuck to the latest news and happenings. If one or the other did want to say something personal they wrote *private* in the subject line.

Mark handed Vicki a stick of gum, and she thanked him. Vicki couldn't remember the last time she had had a mint or gum. Mark had kept a stash of candy from their trip to the GC warehouse and doled it out at appropriate times. Mark loved giving Ryan candy, and he had become one of the child's favorites.

Vicki stuffed the gum in her mouth and thought of her parents. Her dad had chewed this type of gum on Sunday mornings. She remembered him walking into her bedroom with a fresh minty smell on his breath, asking, pleading with her to come with them to church.

"Sun will be coming up in another hour or so," Marshall said, breaking the silence in the car.

"How much farther to Wanda's place?" Vicki said.

Tom studied Mark's notes. "Wanda didn't give mileage, but from where her place used to be, we have to be close."

"What's our plan?" Mark said.

Tom turned. "We find my boy and—" He squinted out the back window. Something flickered in his eyes.

"What is it?" Vicki said, turning.

"We've got company," Tom said.

Lights flashed in the distance, and a GC squad car approached.

"You think they've seen us?" Vicki said.

"Everybody, hang on," Marshall said. "We're pulling into this field, but I won't be able to use my brakes."

When the squad car came over a hill and reached a dip in the road, Marshall took his foot off the accelerator and turned the wheel sharply, sending them into a field. Mark gripped Vicki's shoulder and pulled her down as the car plunged over an embankment.

After the car came to a stop a few yards into the field, Marshall turned off the engine. "Everybody all right?"

Everyone said they were, then watched breathlessly as the GC squad car approached. Vicki closed her eyes and breathed a brief prayer as the squad car sped past and continued east. When it turned a corner, Marshall started the car and pulled back onto the road.

"Wonder where that guy was going in such a hurry," Mark said.

"Call Conrad and ask if he's heard from Wanda," Marshall said. "I don't like seeing the GC on the prowl."

Tom shook his head a few minutes later. "No return message yet."

Mark groaned and put a hand to his forehead. "Why would Cheryl do this? She knows she's putting us in danger."

"Sounds like she's had kind of a meltdown," Marshall said. "Having the baby, then placing it in the Fogartys' house did her in. She's not thinking rationally."

"Does that mean she's not a believer anymore?" Mark said.

No one spoke.

Finally, Vicki broke the silence. "God hasn't abandoned her. Cheryl's turned her back on what she knows is true and good. I think she'll come around—"

"When the GC catch her and chop her head off?" Tom said. His face was red. "And what about my son? What happens when they give him one of those Nicolae tattoos? What's God going to do with that?"

The thought of little Ryan getting the mark of Carpathia frightened Vicki. Judd had told her about Chang Wong and how he had been drugged and given the mark against his will. Surely God wouldn't hold a little one like Ryan responsible for getting the mark. But the GC would make an example of him, parading him in front of the cameras, pleased that they had taken him from the clutches of the evil Judah-ites.

"We're going to get to her before they do anything to him," Vicki said. "Trust me."

"I hope you're right," Tom said.

"And what do we do with Cheryl after we catch her?" Mark said. "She's a threat to the whole group."

"We just **have** to keep praying for her," Vicki said. "That's all we can do."

Tom settled in his seat. "As far as I'm concerned, I don't want that girl within a hundred miles of my family."

The group drove toward glimmers of flashing lights ahead. Finally, they slowed near a decaying gas station on the outskirts of a town. Two sets of lights flickered against a building in the distance, but Vicki couldn't see the GC car.

"From these directions," Tom said, "it looks like we can turn left here and take the back road to Wanda's."

Marshall stroked his stubbly beard and glanced in the rearview mirror. "I don't know about you guys, but I'd like to see what those GC caught."

"Same here," Mark said.

Vicki nodded.

Tom pointed at the gas station and suggested they pull behind it. Quietly they all got out, but Tom told Mark and Vicki to wait.

Mark rolled his eyes and got back in the

car. "I hate it when older people treat you like a kid."

"They're both stressed about Ryan. It's nothing personal."

"Yeah, well, I still liked it better when we called our own shots. The most exciting thing we've done since coming to Avery is go to that warehouse, and we had to sneak around to do that."

Vicki noticed a lightening in the clouds peeking over the horizon. "We have to get to Wanda's quickly if we want to beat the daylight."

Mark tapped his fingers against the armrest, and Vicki strained to see around the back of the gas station. Another GC squad car approached, then passed the station and turned down a street a few blocks away.

Minutes passed and their friends didn't return. "Maybe they found something," Mark said.

The phone rang and Vicki answered. It was Conrad. "Hold on for this one, Vicki. You're not going to believe it. Zeke and I have been watching reports along the East Coast, and some weird stuff is going on. People are getting burned up. GC and anybody with the mark of Carpathia is at risk."

"What do you mean, burned up?"

"Hang on—we're getting onto Dr. Ben-

Judah's Web site. Okay, here it is." He paused, reading through the material. "Does the fourth Bowl Judgment ring a bell?"

Vicki thought a moment. "Wait, isn't that the one where the angel is given power to burn people with fire?"

"Bingo. And it looks like it's happened everywhere the sun's shining. Do you realize what this means?"

"A lot of people are going to die."

"Yeah, but if believers aren't affected, which is what I assume from what I've read of Dr. Ben-Judah's letter, we'll be able to move around during the day."

"What's Conrad want?" Mark said.

"Conrad, thanks. I'll get back to you."

Vicki explained what Conrad had told her and looked toward the horizon. For so long, the sun had caused fear among believers. Now they might not have to be scared of daylight.

"It's been twenty minutes," Mark said. "I think we ought to see what's going on."

"Let's wait another five minutes—"

"Fine, you can stay where you are, but I'm going."

Vicki got out with Mark, switching the phone to vibrate. They stayed away from the street, walking in the same direction as Marshall and Tom, and cut through a hedge.

A dog barked in the distance as they skirted a fence and crept through an open area. A few houses were scattered about—some abandoned, others well kept.

The squad-car lights became brighter, but there was still no sign of Marshall or Tom.

A two-story apartment building loomed before them. They walked to the right, stepping gingerly past old barbecues and gardening tools stacked at the end of the building. They stayed low, creeping onto the scene like two cats searching for prey. Mark dropped to his knees, and Vicki followed as they crawled to the top of a knoll and spotted the squad cars near a van.

A child cried out, and Vicki recognized Ryan. The officers had Cheryl against the front of the van, her hands cuffed behind her. A little farther up the street two officers laughed and pointed at something on the ground. Vicki crawled five feet to her left and gasped. Marshall and Tom lay facedown in the street, their hands behind them.

FOUR

The Chase

VICKI focused on Ryan, who was still inside the van and being cared for by a female officer. The child cried for his mama and struggled with the officer.

"It's okay," Cheryl yelled, tears streaming down her face. "We're going to be okay."

One of the officers near Tom and Marshall keyed his radio. "Two males, one female, and one child. All unmarked."

Vicki wondered if Tom or Marshall had IDs on them. If the GC found out Tom was a former GC officer, they'd take him in for questioning.

Vicki's heart wrenched every time Ryan cried out. She wanted to rush in and grab him but couldn't.

"They must have jumped Tom and

Marshall," Mark whispered. "What do you want to do?"

Vicki glanced at the sky. It would still be a few minutes before the sun rose. "Let me pull the car around. I'll get their attention and see if they take the bait."

"What'll you do if they follow?"

"I'll try to lead them into the light. You see what you can do for Tom and the others."

"Maybe I should take the car—"

"No. You'll be better at helping them. Let me go." Vicki scooted backward quietly and ran to the car. The keys were still in the ignition, and Vicki started it and pulled onto the road. She had the sick feeling that perhaps the plague of burning fire wouldn't hit Wisconsin like it had the rest of the world. Could it be over? If so, Vicki and the others were in deep trouble.

Vicki pulled slowly onto the main road and looked at the surrounding hills. The town lay in a valley, so until the sun was higher, there would be patches of shade throughout the area. She stopped in the middle of the road and focused on trees on the ridge. A thin trail of smoke rose like a white snake. Was it some kind of illusion? or dust? The longer she looked, the more convinced she became that it was smoke.

Vicki rolled her window down, peering up at the eerie sight. A spark, then a flash of fire broke out at the tops of trees. As sunlight spread farther, more leaves and branches were caught in the blaze.

A voice brought Vicki back to reality. "You want to step out of the car, miss?"

A man in uniform stood a few feet in front and to the left of Vicki's car. She hadn't heard him approach, and her heart raced wildly when he took a step closer. "Keep your hands where I can see them and get out—"

Vicki punched the accelerator and threw herself flat on the seat. A gun fired and glass shattered, but she kept her foot down, one hand on the steering wheel. She peeked over the dashboard in time to see she was headed for the curb and swerved as another shot smashed the back windshield, the bullet crashing into the car radio.

As Vicki reached the street where the van was stopped, two GC officers pointed their guns and fired, the other rushing to his car. Vicki ducked again and floored it, hoping none of them would shoot her tires.

She made it past the first few houses and looked up. Before her stretched a wide-open road that led toward the hillside.

Mark waited until he heard the first shot.
The GC radio went crazy when the officer
reported another unmarked citizen nearby.
Mark counted four officers firing as Vicki
passed. The female officer carried Ryan away
from the van and placed him on the ground
near Tom and Marshall.

As the other officers roared away in two of
the squad cars, the female officer walked
back to Cheryl, and Mark saw his chance. He
raced down a slight embankment, careful to
keep the van between him and the officer.
Cheryl screamed for Ryan.

He reached the back of the van and knelt
as the officer pushed Cheryl toward Tom and
Marshall. Mark breathed a quick prayer. He
wasn't sure what to do, but something told
him to get Ryan first.

He duck-walked to the squad car, which
was still running, and reached through the
open window. He tried to throw the car into
gear, but it wouldn't go. He glanced back and
noticed Marshall had seen him.

"There's something crawling on my legs!"
Marshall yelled at the officer. "Come over
here and get it off!"

Mark quietly opened the door, got in,
pushed the brake pedal, and put the car in

drive. The car moved slowly forward as he
scampered away.

As soon as Mark was hidden from view,
Marshall shouted, "Hey, looks like your car's
going on a trip!"

The officer cursed, and Mark heard footsteps
approaching. When the woman passed, he
sprinted toward his friends. Mark raced with
lightning speed toward Ryan and with one
swoop gathered the boy up and darted away.

"Marky!" Ryan said as they ran. The boy
giggled, and Mark tried to quiet him. Finally,
he put a hand over Ryan's mouth. Mark
rushed behind a garage and peered out long
enough to see that the female officer had
stopped the car. Mark held Ryan tight while
he rushed for the abandoned gas station.

Vicki gunned the engine and flew toward the
hills. She couldn't see the sun yet, but she
could see its effect. A trail of smoke rose from
the top of the ridge. If she could reach the
curve above her, which looked no more than
two miles away, she had a chance.

She flicked on her lights and kept an eye on
the rearview mirror. Racing out of the small
town were two squad cars, lights flashing.

Vicki sped up and hit a curve at full speed,

her tires dropping off the edge of the pavement, then hopping back on. The squad cars
gained ground, so she mashed her foot to the
floor and flew down the sloping road and
toward the hill. She had to slow to make the
next curve, and the car bogged down and the
engine revved.

A squad car pulled in directly behind her
and another raced beside her. She glanced to
her left quickly enough to see there was only
one officer in the car. Sirens blared, and
someone on a bullhorn ordered her to pull
over. Vicki kept her hands glued to the steering wheel and looked to her right. The hill
still blocked the sunlight.

"Pull over now!" an officer shouted.

Mark gasped for air and held Ryan tightly
against his chest. The boy had giggled as
Mark ran from the scene, as if they were playing a game. "Candy," Ryan said.

Mark handed him a soft piece of candy
and patted the child's back as they reached
the gas station. He expected to see the squad
car speed toward them at any moment.

"Marky!" Ryan said, looking around.

"Yeah, Marky's here. Now we need to be
really quiet."

Ryan put his hand out. "Blankie! Uh . . .
uh! Blankie!"

"We're going to get your blanket, but we
need to be quiet, okay?"

Ryan wrinkled his nose. "Blankie . . ."

Mark wished he could have helped Tom
and Marshall, but there wasn't time. And if
Conrad was right about the heat plague, he
wouldn't have to stay hidden long before the
GC officers realized the wrath of God.

The gas station was padlocked. Even the rest
rooms around the back were sealed shut. If
anyone came out of their houses or happened
to drive by, he and Ryan would be seen.

"Hey," someone whispered.

Mark looked around. On a hillside were a
few houses. On the other side was a vacant
lot with weeds and bushes.

"Over here," a man said.

Mark focused on what looked like a
manhole cover that was slightly open. A
hand waved Mark forward. Could it be a GC
trick? If so, why would the GC be hiding
underground?

Mark looked at the street. No squad car.
He hugged Ryan tightly and made a run for
the hole. The cover swung open, and a man
with a scraggly beard reached out for the boy.

Ryan grabbed Mark's neck and whined. "Scared! Scared!"

"It's okay, buddy. I'm with you."

Vicki heard the ping of bullets off the back of her car and swerved to her right. The car shook, and she smelled something like rubber burning. A glance in the side mirror showed smoke rising from the car. The GC had shot one of her tires.

As she slowed, Vicki noticed sunshine creeping around the mountain. She floored the accelerator and pulled forward as far as she could. When she stopped, the front half of her car was in sunshine, the back in shadows.

"Get out and lay facedown on the pavement!" a GC officer barked.

Vicki opened the door, her hands in front of her. When she closed the door, one of the officers cursed and yelled for her to get down. Immediately Vicki felt a rise in temperature, not unbearable, but definitely hotter.

She lay down, her face near the pavement. The tar bubbled slightly. As a girl, she had ridden her bike on hot asphalt, and this reminded her of the sticky tar on her shoes and tires at the end of the day.

"I'm unarmed," Vicki said. "There's no reason to shoot."

"Shut up!" an officer shouted.

A man with a dark mustache keyed his radio, calling their partner who had been left behind. "We have the runner. Everything okay back there?"

A female officer spoke, her voice shaky. "The girl and two men are still here, but I've lost the kid."

"What do you mean, you lost him?"

"My squad car must have slipped into gear while I put him down. When I got back he was gone."

"I'm heading back there," Officer Mustache said to the other two.

"All three of you'd better leave," Vicki said.

Officer Mustache turned, his hand on his pistol. "I thought we told you to be quiet."

Vicki pushed herself to a sitting position on the hot pavement and noticed that where her shadow fell, the pavement remained cool. "Has the GC contacted you about what's going on with the sun?"

The three looked at each other but didn't respond. Vicki pulled her knees to her chest. Trees on the other side of the road sizzled and popped. "You hear that? When the sun reaches you and your cars, what's happened all over the world is going to happen to you."

"What's she talking about?" a younger officer said.

"You see how this road is bubbling? Look at the smoke behind me on the hillside. There's something going on here, and you guys had better pay attention."

"Cuff her and bring her back to town," Officer Mustache said.

The younger officer moved toward Vicki, pulling handcuffs from his belt. As he got closer, he stared at the bubbling asphalt. "Sir, this tar over here is—"

But Officer Mustache was already in his car, backing away and speeding down the hill.

The younger officer glanced at the trees. Every minute the sunshine inched closer.

"Go ahead and cuff her and get her in the car," the older officer said.

"What if she's right about the sun? You know we had that report from the East Coast before we left the station."

"Just cuff her and we'll get out of here."

The younger officer walked toward Vicki, his face contorted. He took a step into the sunshine and lifted his boot. Hot, gooey tar stuck to it.

"Stand up and move over here," the officer said.

Vicki remained seated. The officer threw the handcuffs to her and told her to put them on.

"You'll have to come over here and get me," Vicki said.

"Go get her," the older officer shouted.

The younger man pursed his lips, hesitated, then walked into the light. At first he didn't seem to have a problem, other than the sticky road. But when Vicki handed the cuffs to him, he screamed and dropped them.

Frightened, the man turned to his partner, holding his hand in front of him. "She made those handcuffs hotter than fire. It left a mark on my hand!"

"This is the fourth Bowl Judgment," Vicki said. "The Bible says if you're following the evil ruler of this world, you're going to be scorched with fire."

The other officer marched toward Vicki rolling his eyes. He was wearing a short-sleeved shirt, and when he reached to retrieve the handcuffs, a blister raised on his forearm. The man cursed and moved into the shadows, rubbing his arm and sneering. "I hate your God and his plagues! No wonder Nicolae wants you and the rest of your kind dead."

The officer reached for his gun and pulled

it from its holster. By now the sun had moved forward, and the officers had to step back. Vicki scrambled to the other side of her car as the man fired.

"Come on," the younger officer said. "Let's get out of here before it's too late."

The officers hurried to the car and backed away, tires squealing.

Vicki breathed a sigh of relief. It would be a long day for the GC in Wisconsin.

FIVE

Mark's New Friend

MARK crawled into the darkened hole and down rickety stairs. The man inside looked like a castaway from a deserted island. His clothes were dirty and tattered, his beard long enough to touch his chest, and his skin pale.

"You're takin' a big risk out there in daylight without the mark," the man said. "Is this your little brother?"

Mark studied the man's forehead, but there was no mark of the believer or of Nicolae. "No, this is Ryan. The GC stopped his mom just up the street."

"I knew you wasn't GC," the man said. "Come with me."

Ryan clung to Mark's neck as they walked through the room, ducked their heads, and went into another. Mark's eyes adjusted to the dim light, provided by some sort of lamp system around the room.

"Feels like it's gettin' hot out there," the man said. "I've seen the reports."

"What reports?" Mark said.

The man ran a hand over a computer and wiped dust from the screen. "I have to clean everything about once a day." He flicked the computer on and called up images he had saved. Fires engulfed buildings along the East Coast. Scenes of horror Mark could never have imagined flashed, and Mark turned so Ryan couldn't see.

"I expect the same thing's gonna happen here, you think?"

"I'm pretty sure it is."

"Then we need to get your friends off the street, or they'll get burned up."

"There's only one way to make sure we don't get burned," Mark said. "What's your name?"

"Clemson Stoddard," he said, reaching a hand out. "I've been down here since the start of the big war. I was scared of the nuclear stuff at first, but then I kind of liked being out of sight. You're one of the first visitors I've had in ages."

"What is this place?" Mark said.

"There used to be an oil-change place behind the garage. They leveled it after the disappearances, but since I owned the land, I just sealed it up without anybody knowing. Lamps are kerosene. I tapped onto an electric line for my computer and the freezer. Got enough food down here to feed you and your friends for quite a while."

"Why haven't you taken Carpathia's mark?"

Clemson scowled. "He's creepy, don't you think? All that coming back from the dead business. Killin' people for not puttin' one of his tattoos on. I'm gonna ride this one out— that's what I'm going to do."

"Have you seen anything about Dr. Ben-Judah on the Web?"

"Yeah, I've read some of his stuff. I don't mind tellin' ya I'm not into religion. I try to live a good life and help people, but I don't go in much for church and all that Jesus stuff, if you know what I mean."

Vicki watched the squad car race down the hill and take the turns way too fast. She thought the car would flip, but the driver slowed enough around curves to keep it on the road. Up ahead, the sun cast a golden glow. The car sped up to a frightening speed, but before it could reach the shade of some trees ahead, it spun out. From Vicki's perch she saw little puffs of smoke come from each tire.

The squad car came to rest in the middle of the road, blocking both lanes. To her horror, a large truck pulling a huge tank bore down on them from the other direction. The truck tried to stop, but its tires were melting before her eyes, the wheels sliding on the road like melting chocolate donuts.

The two officers jumped from their vehicle a second before the truck collided with the car. An explosion rocked the valley, sending a ball of flame into the air, and the officers fell. One finally stood, thrusting a fist toward the sky before his body was consumed in flames.

Vicki fell to her knees in horror. She covered her face as the smoke and smell of the fire reached her. "God, help me get back to Ryan and Cheryl and the others and let them be all right."

Mark knew Clemson was in serious trouble. He had avoided the Global Community and stayed out of sight from others in the town, but he had no protection from the plagues. Mark discovered the man had been stung by one of the locusts, which had entered through an air vent, but he had obviously avoided the deadly horsemen and hadn't been affected by the wrath of the Lamb earthquake.

"Look, I need to tell you some important stuff, things that will save your life, but I have to check on my friends. Would you mind keeping my little buddy here until I get back?"

"Not a problem," Clemson said. He pulled out a pack of gum and held it up.

"He's too young for that. He just swallows it."

"Right. Well, let me think what else I have here. . . ."

"Do you sing?" Mark said.

Clemson furrowed his brow. "What kind of question is that?"

"He likes 'Twinkle, Twinkle, Little Star' and 'Hush, Little Baby.' "

"Twinkle!" Ryan said.

Clemson laughed, the corners of his eyes wrinkling with delight. "I can give you my country version of that, if you don't mind. Maybe even a little 'You Are My Sunshine'?"

"Sunshine!" Ryan said.

Ryan went to Clemson with his arms outstretched. He seemed fascinated with the

man's long beard and pulled at it. "You
know how long it's been since I laughed out
loud, little guy?"

"Thanks for doing this," Mark said, "but I
have to warn you. Don't go outside. Don't
even go near the opening. The sun's going to
be really hot, and it'll no doubt burn you."

"We'll be all right."

When Mark opened the trapdoor, sunlight
flooded into the hidden room. He smelled
smoke and heard dry weeds crackling. The
last thing he heard before he closed the
trapdoor was the warbly sound of Clemson's
voice softly singing "Twinkle, Twinkle, Little
Star."

Vicki jogged down the hillside as the sun
came over the mountain. She expected everything to burst into flames around her, but it
didn't. A small stream flowing past the road
bubbled and hissed as steam rose, but trees
only a few yards away seemed unaffected.
Plastic mailboxes melted and pooled on the
ground, basketball backboards wilted like
dead flowers, and electric lines strung overhead snapped. Vicki had to be careful that
she didn't go near any of the downed wires
or get hit by falling debris.

Rushing toward town, she noticed another eerie sound overhead. She finally spotted an airplane flying just over the tops of some trees. With its wings on fire, the small plane looked like it was trying to land. Suddenly, the engine's whine stopped, a wing broke off, and the aircraft plunged. It disappeared in some trees, and another explosion rocked the hillside.

Vicki wiped sweat from her forehead and kept running.

Mark made it to the street where Tom, Marshall, and Cheryl sat and gasped when the female officer pointed her gun at them. Buildings behind the woman blocked the sunshine, but from the sweat stains on the woman's shirt, Mark knew she was feeling the heat. A GC squad car squealed to a stop near the group, and a mustached officer jumped out, yelling at the woman. Mark wasn't close enough to hear, but he figured the man knew they had only a few minutes to get away. *But where's Vicki?*

The woman keyed her radio and called for the other officers, but they didn't answer.

Suddenly, a huge explosion rocked the valley, and a plume of smoke and fire rose into the sky from the east. Mark was close enough now to hear some of the conversation. It sounded like Marshall Jameson and Tom Fogarty were urging the GC officers to find shelter in one of the nearby buildings.

A buzzing from overhead distracted the group, and Mark saw a small plane with its wings on fire trying desperately to land. It disappeared behind the buildings, and seconds later they heard the explosion.

"This must be another judgment from God!" Marshall said. "You need to get out of here—"

"You want us to leave so you can get away," Officer Mustache said. "All of you get up and into the car now."

Something on the hillside distracted Mark. An empty car burst into flames, sending a shower of sparks into the air. Mark panicked. He knew his friends were protected from the plague, but what if they were in a car with unbelievers?

Before he could do anything, the two officers had all three of his friends in the back of the squad car. A house on the hillside crackled, and the roof began to smoke.

Mark moved to his left, toward the main road. When the car was a few yards away, he ran into the road and waved wildly. The squad car was in sunlight, and Mark was afraid it might explode.

Officer Mustache honked his horn and swerved, trying to avoid hitting Mark, but Mark moved right in the car's path. The man slammed on his brakes and stopped a few inches away. Sweat poured from the man's face.

The female officer gasped for air, threw the door open, and drew her gun. "On the ground!" she screamed, her gun pointed at Mark's chest. Suddenly, she dropped the weapon and danced on the pavement like a child running from the tide at the beach. Her ponytail bounced behind her while she ran away from the car in circles. Finally, her hair sprouted flames, and she glowed like a human blowtorch.

Officer Mustache exited the car and immediately put a hand over his head. Sparks flew from his mustache, and he fell and rolled.

Mark turned away, unable to watch. The officers' screams faded quickly as their bodies were consumed. Mark opened the back doors, and his friends scooted out.

Vicki came upon the squad car and her four friends and couldn't help crying. The two GC officers lay at the side of the road in ash heaps. Vicki wiped away her tears and found the keys to the handcuffs near the female's body. Vicki released Cheryl, Tom, and Marshall before turning to Mark. "Where's Ryan?"

"Come on. I'll show you."

They walked in silence through the town. A few streets over they heard screaming as more fires broke out. Vicki felt like she was walking through the fiery furnace, like the three Old Testament believers Shadrach, Meshach, and Abednego. But this was no furnace—it was the real world burning at the hand of an angry God. Vicki couldn't help but think of hell. She knew there were some who believed it wasn't a real place, but the more she looked around, the more she was convinced that the Bible was true and that hell had to exist.

Mark led them to Clemson's hideout and opened the trapdoor. Vicki heard singing inside and smiled when she realized Ryan was picking up the words to "You Are My Sunshine."

Vicki caught Cheryl's arm and told the others to go inside. Cheryl pulled away and said she needed to see Ryan.

"We need to talk first," Vicki said.

Cheryl nodded and turned as Vicki closed the entrance. They walked to the middle of the empty lot, and Cheryl folded her arms. "I know what you're going to say, and I deserve whatever it is you guys have decided to do."

"We haven't decided to *do* anything yet. I want to hear it from you—why did you lie to Wanda and take Ryan?"

Cheryl sat in the dirt and buried her head in her hands. "I was so jealous of what Josey had with Ryan. I had done all the work and had gone through all the pain, and she was getting the reward. That little boy was part of me. I felt him growing inside me. Being that close to him was just torture."

"We never should have let you stay that close to him," Vicki said. "If I had it to do over again, I'd have gone with you to another location."

"Where?" Cheryl said. "I don't want to be anywhere but with Ryan."

Vicki kept quiet as Cheryl cried. She had hoped Cheryl would say she was sorry for taking Ryan, but she seemed to be making excuse after excuse.

"Being cooped up at that camp didn't help. There's nothing to do, and every time I saw Ryan I thought about us being together, just him and me. That's how it should have been."

"How did you plan it?"

"The van? I watched Marshall and figured

out where he kept his keys. It took a while, but I finally got them. All that time I planned where I would go. At first, I was going to just drive and ask God to show me a place. Then I got scared and decided to write Wanda."

"We found your e-mails to her."

Cheryl smacked her forehead. "I thought I'd deleted those."

"Cheryl, you made a promise to Josey and Tom. You know you can't give Ryan the kind of home—"

"I'm his mother! There's only a little more than a year before Jesus comes back, and I can do as much for him as anybody."

"I think you've ruined that now. How can we trust you when you kidnap—"

"My own son?"

"When you get so moody and won't talk and then endanger all of us by kidnapping a member of the group?"

Vicki watched Cheryl stare at the fires raging on the hillside. She didn't know what to say and silently prayed, "God, please show Cheryl where's she's been wrong. Help her to see the truth about what she's done and admit her mistakes. And give us wisdom with what to do with her. Amen."

SIX

Clemson's Decision

JUDD Thompson Jr. and Lionel Washington walked out of their Ohio hideout in daylight for the first time since they had arrived. It was difficult convincing others that it was safe to venture out. When everyone read Dr. Ben-Judah's latest message and heard what was going on around the world, they finally let Judd and Lionel go.

Judd uncovered the Humvee, and the two headed away from the hiding place. They were in a remote area, so it took them a few minutes to reach a town, but when they did, Judd wished they hadn't come.

They crossed a river that bubbled like someone was boiling macaroni. The Humvee was engulfed in white-hot steam, then quickly passed through to the other side. They sped by a brick school, smoke billowing through open windows. Playground equipment lay bent and twisted, melting from the intense heat that neither Lionel nor Judd could feel. To them, it seemed like a hot summer day in Chicago, not the inferno that unbelievers felt.

The sky was cloudless so the sun beat down. The normally light blue heavens reflected an orange-yellow from fires on the ground. Homes and businesses smoked and smoldered, threatening fire at any moment.

Judd saw no airplanes or choppers above them. He wondered what a large airport would look like with fires breaking out on grounded planes. *What an awful smell boiling blood must be in the oceans*, he thought.

In a residential section of town, Lionel pointed out finely manicured lawns that had turned from deep green to brown as the grass went up in flames.

They neared a convenience store and slowed when the roof began to curl under the oppressive heat. Huge windows in front burst, spreading glass all the way to the street. Judd backed up a safe distance as hoses to gas pumps melted. A few minutes later the whole thing exploded.

"How is anybody surviving this?" Lionel said.

Judd shook his head. "I guess they have to get underground. But a lot of people in basements are going to have their houses fall on them."

Judd saw a fire department's door open, and an engine rushed out. Firefighters in full gear bounced inside as the truck rolled onto the street. But as soon as the engine hit the street, GC flags on the truck burst into flames. Firefighters flailed their arms and struggled against their seat belts. The red truck slowed, its massive tires melting and spreading onto the pavement. First the driver, then the rest abandoned ship, running toward the fire-house. Before they reached the driveway, they burst into flames. One firefighter ran to the back, managed to turn the water on, and pointed the hose toward his coworkers. Boil-ing water scalded his friends. They screamed and fell before catching on fire.

Lionel trembled. "It's not even the hot part of the day, and people are dying. Any idea how long this will last?"

"We don't know. Let's get back to the hide-out and figure out when to head north."

Mark had learned a long time ago that a per-son didn't become a believer in God simply because of information, so he had to resist the urge to spell everything out for Clemson.

Instead, he asked Clemson about his family, where he had grown up, and his church background.

"I've never been too big on church. My parents went, but I didn't want anything to do with it. I've always felt the Lord knows a person without them having to get dressed up in fancy clothes and making a big show."

"Did you lose anybody in the disappearances?"

"Yeah, lots of people wound up missing. I lived with my mother back then, taking care of her. She was usually up and cookin' breakfast each morning, listenin' to the radio preachers and singin' gospel songs. But that day it was just as quiet as a graveyard. I went out to the pump house to get some apple butter for my toast, and I checked on her, thinkin' somethin' might have happened. Well, you know what I found. Her bed was empty."

"What do you think happened?"

Clemson stroked his beard and picked up a picture of an older woman with shoulder-length hair. "To this day, I don't know what to think. I guess it could have been some kind of sign from God, but I don't know." He paused. "What do you think?"

Mark ran a hand through his hair. He didn't want to preach, but he didn't want to hold back either. "My friends and I have found out that God really exists and that he cares for each of us. In fact, he cared so much that he predicted everything that's happening right now."

"Even this heat wave?"

Mark nodded. "He predicted there would be a ruler that would arise who would lead people away from the truth—"

"Carpathia. I think he's the Antichrist."

"You're right. And the Bible predicted the worldwide earthquake, the stinging locusts—"

"I hated them things. . . ."

"—and even that people would reject his truth, in spite of all the miraculous signs."

"I don't reject anything God does. I believe we all ought to live by the Golden Rule and love others. I've prayed to God before."

"What did you say?"

Clemson shrugged. "I asked him for food and to help me find a safe place to stay, that kind of thing."

"Did he answer?"

Clemson wiped his forehead with a hand-kerchief. "Sure did. There's lots of people who've been carted off by the GC from around here or who have turned in people without the mark for the reward. I've been protected."

Mark drew closer and got down on one

knee. "Clemson, it's not enough just to believe that God exists. The Bible says that the demons believe that. Even Carpathia believes in God."

"I don't think God cares about an old boy like me. He's got plenty to think about without worrying about my troubles."

"So God's not big enough to care for you? To help you find food and shelter?"

"I don't know. . . ."

"The reason we came here was to find that little boy in the next room. But I think God had a bonus in mind." Mark squinted. "Have you been asking God for anything lately?"

"Such as?"

"A sign? Maybe some help? Praying that if God's real, he'd show you and send somebody?"

The man turned white. "How did you know that?"

"I didn't. It was a guess. But since we've found you, I figured God had prepared the way."

Clemson walked to the other side of the room and sat on a rickety stool. "It gets kind of lonesome. I had a dog that stayed with me, but he died about a year ago. He used to stay right beside me like he was scared of what was going on outside." His smile faded. "Bein' all alone gets you to thinking, and I guess over the past few months I've been wonderin' whether or not God was up there and if he cared about all the people dyin'. You think he does?"

"I think the reason that all this bad stuff has happened is that God cares more than any of us can imagine. He wants people to come to know him, to ask forgiveness for their sins, even though he knows that most people will spit in his face."

"Well, if you're so religious why are you still here?"

"One of the reasons he's left us here is so we could reach out to people and help them come to know Jesus personally." Mark told his story briefly, how he had become a true believer in Jesus after the disappearances and had joined the Young Tribulation Force. "I thought I knew God before all this happened, and I thought a lot of other people were just playing church. Some were. But most of my friends who asked me to go to church with them had something I didn't have."

"And what was that?"

"They knew they were forgiven by God because of what Jesus did on the cross. You see, he died so that you could live forever with God and so that you could have a relationship with him right now."

Vicki, Marshall, and Cheryl walked quietly into the room, and Clemson looked up. "And it happened the same way with you people?"

"My parents were these religious nutcases," Vicki said. "They wanted me to go to church with them and read my Bible. I thought Christians were just people who didn't want to have any fun. Now I know the truth, that you can have *real* life, something that lasts, if you give your life to God."

Clemson stared at the floor. "From what I can gather, you people came searching for that little boy because one of you ran off with him. How did that happen?"

No one spoke for a long time. Finally, Cheryl folded her arms and her chin quivered. "Just because we believe in God doesn't mean we'll always make the right decisions." She looked at Vicki and frowned. "I made a big mistake. I can see that now. And there's nothing I can do to make up for it. But I know God is in the business of forgiving people."

Mark looked at Clemson squarely. "Would you like to ask God to forgive you and ask him to come into your life?"

Clemson rubbed his neck with a hand. "I don't know. This has all come on kind of sudden-like. I need some time."

"I understand. But we have to head back, and you need to know that if you go outside during the day without God's protection, you'll die. It's as simple as that."

"I can't make this decision just because I want to live longer."

"Right," Mark said. "But there's no guarantee you'll be alive tomorrow. Half the people in the world have already died. Most of those who were stung by locusts cursed God. But you've been given a second chance. All of us have, and we want to urge you to take it right now."

Tom Fogarty came into the room with Ryan. The child was humming a crude version of "Jesus Loves Me," and Clemson smiled. "I swear it'd be worth it just to have that kid around. There hasn't been much to smile about the past few years."

Mark held out his hands, and Ryan came to him. "Jesus once called a small child over to him and put the kid right in front of the people he was talking to." Mark stood Ryan in front of Clemson, then clicked on the kids' Web site and found the verse he was looking for. "Jesus said, 'I assure you, unless you turn from your sins and become as little children, you will never get into the Kingdom of Heaven. Therefore, anyone who becomes as humble as this little child is the greatest in the Kingdom of Heaven.' "

"What's that mean, exactly?" Clemson said.

"A little kid depends on others. Ryan can't do much on his own. But he trusts us to take care of him, feed him, and help him. God wants you to put that kind of trust in him."

"I said I didn't want to go to church because it was a show," Clemson said. "The truth is, most of those people in church knew what kind of things I did. Bad things. And I bet if you knew, you wouldn't be so quick to help me."

"Every one of us in this room has sinned," Mark said. He glanced at Cheryl and noticed she had covered her face with her hands. "Because we're sinners, a holy God can't allow us into his presence. That's why he sent his only Son, Jesus, to die for us on the cross. It was his sacrifice in our place that guarantees our forgiveness if we'll ask for it."

"I've always believed in Jesus, that he was God, you know, but I've never really done anything about it."

"Do it now." Mark showed Clemson more verses from the Bible that spoke of God's love. The one that seemed to click with the man came from Romans:

> *Therefore, since we have been made right in God's sight by faith, we have peace with*

> *God because of what Jesus Christ our Lord
> has done for us. Because of our faith, Christ
> has brought us into this place of highest
> privilege where we now stand, and we
> confidently and joyfully look forward to
> sharing God's glory.*

"So you're saying I can be right with God
and not have to worry about any of this
Carpathia stuff?"

"Becoming a believer doesn't mean all
your problems go away, but as the Bible says,
if God is for you, who can be against you?"

"How do I do this faith thing? Do I have to
jump through some hoops or memorize a
bunch of stuff?"

"There's another verse in Romans you'll
appreciate." Mark called it up on the computer. "Romans 10:13 says, 'Anyone who calls
on the name of the Lord will be saved.' "

"Then I want to do some callin' right
now," Clemson said.

Mark knelt on the dusty floor with the
man. The others gathered around and put a
hand on Clemson's shoulder as he prayed
along with Mark.

"Dear Jesus—"

"Jesus!" Ryan said.

Everyone laughed, and Mark and Clemson

continued. "I come to you now and call on your name in faith. I believe you died in my place on the cross so I could be forgiven. I'm sorry for rejecting you so long, and I ask you now to come into my life and save me. Jesus, I'm sorry for the bad things I've done, and I come to you like a little child, believing that what you've said is true. Take control of me and teach me your ways. You said anybody who calls on your name would be saved, and I believe it. I call on you now, in Jesus' name. Amen."

Clemson stood and gawked at the others. "What's that funny-looking thing on your foreheads?"

SEVEN

Last Leg of the Trip

VICKI was encouraged by the change in Cheryl. Something had happened to the girl as she listened to Mark talk with Clemson. But in a heated meeting with Tom and Marshall, the group agreed Cheryl shouldn't return with them.

Clemson gathered a few of his things and followed the others outside. As the sun rose higher, roofs of buildings curled and fires broke out around them. Vicki saw no animals, no living people, just the rising heat vapor from the charred pavement.

Miraculously, they found the van in perfect condition and began loading Clemson's things inside. Tom had held Ryan the entire time, not even letting the boy get near Cheryl. When they were almost finished loading, Cheryl approached Vicki and asked what the group had decided.

"I don't think going back with us is a good idea," Vicki said. "We'll head to Wanda's and see if you can stay there."

"What if I don't want to stay with her?"

Vicki put an arm around Cheryl. "This isn't easy for any of us. Make the most of this time away, and down the road—"

"What happens if I can't get back down the road? Wanda could turn out to be—"

Tom passed, holding Ryan with one hand and holding the phone to his ear with the other. Ryan smiled and waved at Cheryl. She turned to Vicki. "I'll do anything to see my little boy again."

"Then use this time. Let God work on you."

Cheryl nodded and everyone got in the van.

The drive to Wanda's took thirty minutes. Vicki thought their whole ordeal was worth the look on Wanda's face when she saw Ryan. She couldn't believe how big and healthy he looked.

When Vicki had Wanda alone, she explained the situation with Cheryl, and Wanda gave a worried look. "There are people who depend on me. I'm always happy to help, but if this girl keeps me from doing—"

"I have a good feeling about her," Vicki

interrupted. "I think she's turned a corner, but she needs help."

"I can keep her busy, but it's going to be up to her to want to change."

They talked until the afternoon, and Vicki and the others decided to return to the cabins the next morning. As evening approached, the sun lowered, and Vicki had never seen such a sunset. Smoke from the rising fires mixed with the fading twilight and created a blend of colors that took her breath away. Fiery red clouds were tinged with purple and orange. Vicki wished she had a camera.

When they heard movement on the road, everyone retreated into Wanda's hideout and watched the coverage by the Global Community News Network. Weather authorities tried to explain the killer heat wave, but every theory given by experts made Vicki laugh. Everyone in the world knew God had caused the heat.

Leon Fortunato spoke against Dr. Tsion Ben-Judah's claims that the Bible predicted the plague. "The enemies of world peace will twist these ancient words to fit their own agenda," he said. "His Excellency assures me that this change in weather is only temporary. And we reject reports that there is some god punishing innocent people for simply living their lives. That is not the kind of god I want to serve. I wish to serve the loving, generous god we have come to know, Nicolae Carpathia."

"Interesting that Leon is speaking to us from some underground cavern," Mark said, pointing out the background of the room.

Cameras picked up the effects of the devastation, since no one could photograph the actual burning during the middle of the day. Firefighters had to try and contain the damage to major cities at night and hope the next day things would get back to normal.

Judd was frustrated that he couldn't reach Vicki. The group in Ohio gathered shortly after Judd and Lionel returned from exploring and tapped into a secret feed from the Tribulation Force in San Diego.

Rayford Steele appeared on-screen. "We don't know how much time we're going to have, so we have to work quickly to take advantage of this opportunity. I've spoken personally with Dr. Ben-Judah, and he's given his blessing on our decision to go ahead with this operation.

"We'll need volunteers throughout the country to rearrange our storehouses of goods and products we trade through the International Commodity Co-op. We believe the Global Community and their followers will focus on survival, looking for relief from the sun. From what we can tell, thousands or maybe hundreds of thousands died today. In the coming days, we'd like to hear from believers and find out what help you need. Our goal is to move resources, but if we need to, we'll move people out of harm's way.

"This will not be easy, and it will be dangerous. We have no idea how long the heat wave will last. But we must take advantage of it as quickly as possible."

Judd wrote the Tribulation Force immediately and volunteered. *I'm hoping to be in Wisconsin by the time you need me, but let me know how I can join the effort.*

Judd and Lionel met with the leaders of the Ohio group and talked about how to proceed. Later in the evening Lionel handed Judd the phone and smiled. "The bride-to-be is on the line."

Judd grabbed the phone, and Vicki explained the situation with Cheryl and where they were. "We're going back to the campground in the morning, assuming the plague continues. What about you?"

"The leaders here have given the okay for

us to head your way. They're concerned that with all the fires and debris on the roads, we might not make it in a day, so we're stopping at a midway point for the night.

"I can't believe we're actually going to see each other!"

"I just hope the plague doesn't end in the morning and we run into a bunch of GC officers."

Judd found it difficult to sleep that night. The group posted guards at the main entrance to the hideout and kept a couple of members up all night watching the property. Judd thought it was a miracle that even with the extreme heat, the group's outside cameras hadn't been affected.

There were tearful good-byes the next morning as the sun rose.

"Red sky at morning, GC take warning," Lionel said.

The doctor at the hideout who had helped with Lionel's arm examined it one more time and pronounced him healthy. Judd and Lionel thanked everyone for their help, and two men loaded enough supplies in the Humvee for a week. Another man made sure they had enough fuel, and the two sped off.

The fire's damage shocked Judd as he crossed the old border of Ohio and drove into Indiana. Trees and crops that had been green the last time they were there lay black and scorched. Judd had seen forest fire damage, but this seemed even worse.

Judd swerved to avoid several vehicles that had burned the day before. Even worse than the dead trees, grass, and plant life were the charred bodies that littered the roadway, and Judd saw Lionel cringe several times while they drove.

"What do you miss most about the way things used to be?" Lionel said as they neared a city.

"I miss my parents and my little brother and sister," Judd said. "I think a lot about what they'd be doing if they were here. Marc and Marci would be in high school. But I also miss little things like going to Wrigley Field for a Cubs game or grabbing a burger at a local restaurant. I had dreamed of owning my own car and being my own boss. Going to movies—"

"Yeah, movies," Lionel said as they passed a destroyed theater complex. "The last time I went to a theater was with my sister."

"I know it sounds corny," Judd said, "but I miss just going to a church service too. I didn't like them when I was young, but now I'd give anything to be able to sing together and listen to teaching without being afraid."

"That's why I envy Sam for being in Petra. It must be one big church service every day." Lionel stretched his arm, put his seat back, and smiled. "So, how are you going to court Vicki?"

"Court?" Judd smirked.

"Yeah, what are you two going to do, take a walk in the fire?"

"I'll admit I'm a little worried about it."

"Why?"

"We've been apart so long, and we've both changed. Plus, the last time we were together, we fought like cats and dogs."

Lionel chuckled. "Vicki sure got ticked at you a few times."

"Right. And how do we know we won't keep fighting?"

"Because God's been working on you."

"What do you mean?"

"I've told you this before. I was around you when we first started the Young Trib Force. You were . . . how do I say this . . . bossy. You knew you had the right plan, and anybody who got in your way was wrong."

Judd smiled. "Me?"

"Over the last few months, years even, I've seen God knock some rough edges off. He's humbled you."

"You talk like I was Frankenstein's monster."

"No, more like Frankenstein's selfish son." Lionel laughed. "I'm not saying you're perfect, and I expect you and Vicki are going to knock even more rough edges off each other, but you've come a long way. And I'm proud to be your friend."

"Thanks."

Vicki's heart nearly broke when she watched Cheryl say good-bye to Ryan. Tom let her hold the boy before they left, and Cheryl sang a song she had made up for him. Through her tears she choked out the words and kissed him on the cheek. "I'm really sorry," she said as she handed Ryan to Tom. "Will you tell Mrs. Fogarty that—"

"You should tell her yourself," Tom said. "Write her or call her."

"I will. And I want you to know I'm going to get better. I've never been through anything like this before."

Tom opened the door and carried Ryan outside. Clemson put a hand on Cheryl's shoulder and smiled, showing his yellow teeth. "I don't excuse your behavior, but the truth is, I wouldn't have found God's peace if you all hadn't driven through our town. So I thank you for your part in that."

Cheryl nodded and hugged everyone. "I don't know what I would have done without you," she whispered in Vicki's ear.

"I look forward to having you back, but don't rush it. Talk this through with Wanda. Let God work."

The drive back to the campground went quickly in the daylight. Vicki wondered how many people had died in the houses that smoldered on hillsides. But she couldn't contain her excitement over Judd. She looked out the window and smiled for no reason. Marshall caught her and asked why she was so happy, but she turned and tickled Ryan in his car seat without answering.

Along with the good feelings, Vicki couldn't help being nervous. What if she and Judd didn't get along? Their friendship had grown, but what if things changed when they were face-to-face?

Before the disappearances, the way a guy looked had been so important to her. Whether a guy looked "hot" was the only test Vicki had used to decide whether to go out with him. Now she couldn't imagine being interested in anyone who didn't share her faith in God and want to reach out to others. She was sure there was nothing that would keep her from liking Judd.

Judd and Lionel made it safely to the midway
point of their trip by early afternoon and
thought about continuing but decided to play
it safe. They found the group they had contacted packed into the basement of an old
library and running out of food. Judd and
Lionel took the food they needed from the
Humvee for the rest of their trip and gave the
rest to the group.

"We e-mailed the Trib Force about supplies,
but they don't know when they'll be able to
get here," the leader said.

"I'm hoping to help move supplies
around," Judd said. "I'll put in a word about
your situation."

If Judd had trouble sleeping the night
before, this night was a disaster. One of the
younger members argued with the leader, and
another coughed most of the night. Judd and
Lionel slept on the floor, which was a thin
strip of carpet over a slab of concrete. Judd
walked the floor above them through the early
morning hours, looking out at the charred
remains of cars, trucks, and trees.

Before they left the next morning, Judd
warned the leader about GC movement in
the area. "I didn't see squad cars, but people

were definitely out last night. When they see this library still standing, they may try to take possession of it, so be careful."

The leader thanked them for the food and wished them well on the remainder of their trip. Lionel pulled out the tattered map they had started with in South Carolina so long ago and traced his finger along the route they had carefully chosen for this final leg of the trip. It ran a hundred miles south of Chicago so they wouldn't have to deal with the new GC buildup outside the nuked city.

Judd had to keep from driving too fast on the sweltering roadway. He set the cruise control and let the Humvee keep speed until he came to a burning wreck or a melted bridge. Twice they were forced to drive through a small stream or find another route.

Finally, they reached the road to the campground Vicki had described.

Lionel folded the map and put it in his pocket. "How do you feel?"

Judd took a breath. "Remember when those GC guys were looking for us in Israel? It's like my heart's beating out of my chest."

"Settle down, big boy. It's just another stop on our way to the Glorious Appearing, right?"

"Maybe it is for you," Judd said. He let off on the gas pedal and slowed. "I want to remember this last part of the drive."

EIGHT

Reunion

LIONEL felt a strange mix of emotions as he got out of the Humvee and walked toward the campground. A white van and another car were parked nearby, and he spotted a child's toy in the grass and picked it up.

Lionel had dreamed of this moment from the first time he suggested he and Judd return home. Through trips to New Babylon, France, Petra, and their ordeal in South Carolina, Lionel never let go of the dream of being back with his friends.

But how will they react to my missing arm? The thought sent a shiver through him and Lionel turned. Judd was still in the car, his hands on the steering wheel, peering into the afternoon sunlight. Lionel shook off the emotion and walked toward the first cabin.

The door opened and Conrad flew out,

racing to his friend and embracing him.
Lionel hugged him tightly and wept. Darrion
followed, then Shelly and Mark. The rest was
a blur as familiar faces and people he'd never
seen surrounded him.

"You wouldn't believe how we've prayed
for you," an older woman said. "You look
just like I thought you would."

Lionel smiled and tried to speak.

"I'm Maggie," the woman said. "Vicki and
the others helped me get out of Des Plaines."

A woman holding a child stepped forward,
and Lionel handed her the toy. "Where is
Vicki?"

Zeke stepped forward and grabbed Lionel's
hand. "Vicki and Janie have been down at
Cheryl's cabin fixing the place up. Down at
the end."

Lionel glanced back at the Humvee. Judd
was still inside.

The emotion of seeing Lionel connect with
his friends was too wonderful for Judd. Years
ago, when Judd was a kid, he'd had relatives
visit his family. At the end of the visit there
were hugs and tears as Judd's parents said
good-bye. At that age, Judd couldn't understand why older people cried so much.

Now, as he saw the friendships formed during the earth's last days, he shook with emotion. These people had prayed for him, had faced death together, and had lost many friends. The gathering seemed like a breathtaking dream.

Vicki and Janie had worked on Cheryl's old cabin since Vicki had returned from her trip. Food wrappers littered the floor. Clothes were thrown about, and Cheryl's cot hadn't been made for weeks. Though Marshall had assigned cabins and put at least two people in each (he said the partner system was best), Cheryl had stayed alone, which was fine with everyone else. But Cheryl's solitary life had come with a price. Vicki wondered what might have happened if the girl had roomed with someone who could have helped her think through the situation with Ryan and the Fogartys.

Janie had finished moving a bed into place when Vicki heard a commotion outside. Janie went to the window and noticed several people walking toward the cabin.

"Are they here?" Vicki said.

"Only one way to find out," Janie said,

then rushed out, the screen door banging behind her.

Vicki tried to move but couldn't. "God," she prayed, "you know how long we've prayed for Judd and Lionel to come back. You know all that's happened, so before I even see them, I want to thank you for loving us and sending them back. Whatever happens between Judd and me, even if we just become friends, I pray you'd get the glory for it. Amen."

The screen door opened, and Lionel walked inside. He looked older, his eyes somehow wiser. Vicki had first met Lionel when he was only thirteen. Now he was almost nineteen, and he had grown taller than Vicki by a few inches. She rushed to him and hugged him, forgetting about his arm injury.

"I'm not hurting you, am I?" Vicki said when she could speak.

Lionel smiled. "Nothing there to hurt."

"Oh, Lionel, we've missed you so much. I thought you'd be gone a couple of weeks, maybe a month tops."

"So did I. Guess things don't always turn out the way you think they're going to."

Vicki glanced at the door, and Lionel stepped aside. "Were you looking for somebody else?"

Vicki smiled. "He's with you, isn't he?"

Lionel took her hand and pulled her toward the door. "Come on."

The first one to reach Judd after he stepped out of the car was Mark. There were no words, just hugs and slaps on the back. Judd and Mark had disagreed about a lot of things through the years, beginning with Mark's involvement with the militia movement, but now all that seemed forgotten. They had both seen enough death and had been chased by the Global Community enough to know that any squabbles in the past were easily put aside.

"You don't know how good it is to be back," Judd said.

Zeke gave Judd a hug that nearly squeezed all the air from his lungs. "Looks like you got a few scratches during your travels."

"You haven't changed much, Zeke. Still have the tattoos."

"I'm thinkin' about gettin' a new one here," Zeke said, pointing to his right hand. "It'll be a GC symbol with the words *Carpathia stinks.*"

"Judd!" Shelly screamed. Zeke and Mark made way for her as she embraced Judd.

"It's a big family reunion," Zeke said.

Judd studied the faces outside the cabins while he walked this gauntlet. He recognized Tom and Josey Fogarty and hugged them tightly.

"Vicki told me you'd finally believed," Judd said to Tom.

"It took me a while to come around, but I finally realized the truth."

Darrion pecked Judd on the shoulder. "Remember me?"

Judd couldn't believe how much Darrion had changed. When he had first met her, she was just a kid. Now she was a young woman with long hair and a beautiful smile.

"Everybody's changed so much—it's hard to believe."

"I think there's somebody down there who wants to see you," Darrion whispered. "She's been really nervous."

Judd watched as Lionel came out of a cabin pulling someone behind him.

Vicki stepped outside the cabin and saw the glow on the faces of those before her. Somehow Vicki felt she had seen this moment before or had dreamed it. At the top of the hill, a few yards from the main cabin, a young man moved slowly toward her.

Judd had never felt so focused. He knew everyone was watching, wondering what he would do, but he concentrated on the girl at the end of the path.

Vicki had changed since Judd had been gone, like the others, like he had. Her red hair was shorter, and Judd liked how it accented her face. She looked older, more mature.

On the drive to the airport, shortly after Judd and Vicki had first met in that cataclysmic moment after their families had disappeared, Judd hadn't even considered Vicki as anything but a fellow traveler, a lost and lonely survivor. When everyone he loved was gone, his first instinct was to shut down and keep people at a distance so he wouldn't be hurt even more.

The loss of Bruce Barnes had been another huge blow to Judd. But over the past two years, Judd had opened up to others in a way he had never done before. As he walked past this band of brothers and sisters, he wasn't just returning to his friends—he was truly coming home.

The thought overwhelmed Judd the closer he got to Vicki. Could God have loved him so much to take him safely through the past years and bring him back to the person he loved most? Had his adventures, his fighting the Global Community all been part of a plan to draw him closer to the God who loved him?

Somewhere deep inside, the pride, self-reliance, lack of trust in others, the guarding of his heart, and even the focus on his own sins was breaking down. For so long Judd had tried to figure things out. He knew the Bible, how things would wind up when Christ came back, and how everyone should act and fit in with his views. But the more Judd had tried to control things and people, the worse he felt.

He was a few feet from Vicki when the emotion he was trying to control crashed. He had stayed in the car to compose himself, to keep himself guarded again, but the sight of that old dog Ryan Daley had brought home sent Judd over the edge. Phoenix bounded past Vicki and ran toward Judd, his tail wagging, barking with delight. Judd fell to his knees and put his hands on the ground, tears streaming.

At first Vicki thought Judd had fallen, then realized he was overcome. When Phoenix jumped up and licked his face, Vicki couldn't tell if Judd was laughing or crying.

She knelt and put an arm around Judd's shoulder and the other around Phoenix. Everything else in the world faded—the people around her, the hot sun, all the death and destruction, the Global Community.

Judd whispered something through his tears—she could tell they were tears now. "What did you say?" she said.

"I'm so sorry, Vicki. I'm so sorry."

"It's okay, Judd. You're back. What do you have to be sorry about?"

"For Phoenix. For Ryan. For the way I've been."

Vicki smiled and started to make Judd feel better, but then she realized that God was doing something. Here. Now. God was burrowing into Judd's soul, working in a way she had seen only when a person came to faith in God. To others it probably seemed like Judd was happy to see Vicki, but she sensed something more.

Vicki placed both arms around Judd's neck and whispered a prayer. "Oh, Father, you're so good to us. You've brought my friend back. Thank you."

Judd looked at Vicki, and she handed him a tissue. His face was shadowed by a couple days' growth of beard. He had aged beyond his twenty-one years. Vicki looked at the others gathered around. Josey Fogarty smiled and cradled Ryan tightly in her arms. Zeke had his hand over his mouth, studying the scene. Darrion and Janie and Shelly hugged each other and cried. They had been such good friends for Vicki.

"I'm through with just surviving," Judd choked. "I want to live. Do you think I can change?"

"I think you already have."

First Steps

JUDD had never experienced a celebration like the one that evening in Wisconsin. He had been to birthday parties, anniversaries, and victory celebrations, but they didn't compare with the joy in the main cabin.

Zeke pulled out a boxful of different juices that no one knew he had. "I was waiting for the right time and place, and this is it!"

Josey Fogarty had baked several cakes, which she said was therapy for her. "I hated waiting for word about Ryan, so while I prayed I baked."

"You could have saved the oven and just stuck the cake outside," Zeke laughed.

Ryan couldn't take his eyes off Lionel. He was fascinated with Lionel's skin color and the fact that one of his sleeves was empty. Lionel seemed to take the attention in stride and let Ryan see the way his arm had healed.

Vicki left Judd to talk with Josey. Judd assumed it was to explain what had happened with Cheryl the day before.

After everyone had eaten, Judd asked Vicki if she would like to take a walk before the sun went down.

Zeke stepped in front of Judd, blocking the door. "As Vicki's substitute dad, I'm going to have to ask your intentions."

People snickered.

Judd planted his feet and took a breath. "Sir, I'm here to renew an old friendship, if that's okay with you."

Zeke looked at Vicki. "Are you open to this young man renewing your acquaintance?"

"I am."

"Then go on, but have her back by dark." Zeke leaned forward. "I'm serious about that last part. We've been doing a lot of moving around. I don't want any surprise visits from the GC in the middle of the night."

Vicki led the way, showing Judd each of the cabins and telling him who lived where. She came to Zeke's workshop, which no one visited anymore. "Z's really excited about what he's been working on for Lionel. After the people stopped coming for fake IDs and cosmetic work, he started developing it."

When they had seen all the cabins, Vicki led Judd through the woods a short distance to a knoll overlooking the camp and the surrounding countryside. It seemed like years since Judd had been outside in daylight and he loved it, even if the devastating fires still raged. Smoke hovered over the valley, and in the distance Judd saw houses and farms ablaze.

The fire hadn't touched the woods surrounding the camp, and Judd was amazed. Like the other plagues, this could only be explained by the awesome power of God.

Judd and Vicki sat on a tree stump, side by side, and looked at the scene.

"This world is on its last legs," Vicki said.

"I can't wait to see what the new one's going to look like." Judd shifted nervously. "That wasn't the kind of entrance I'd hoped to make earlier. I had planned a private kind of thing, sneaking up on you and seeing if you'd recognize me."

"You had a lot of time to plan it out," Vicki said.

"I didn't think there would be so many people."

"It was a wonderful way to return."

"Zeke said I really lost it, and I guess I did."

"It's funny how people react to emotion. A lot of people are really uncomfortable, but I don't think you should ever be sorry about that. It was so genuine. I could tell God was doing something special in your heart."

"I used to sit in church and watch people go forward at the end of the service and try to figure out how they got the guts to do it. It seemed so humiliating to get up there in front of all those people, sometimes crying, other times just standing there. But when I saw you and Phoenix, I finally realized what a jerk I've been. I've seen it before, but it was like God showing me wave after wave of truth. I don't feel like a very worthy candidate to be your friend, let alone be . . ."

"What?" Vicki said.

"You know . . . more than that."

Vicki took Judd's hand and squeezed it. "I know we only have a little more than a year left before the Glorious Appearing, but I'd like to take this slow. Get to know each other better. There are things I need to tell you and things I need to hear from you."

Judd nodded. "Where do we start?"

"Tell me about Nada," Vicki said.

Judd did. He spilled the whole story about Nada, from their first meeting to Nada's eventual death in an Israeli jail cell. Vicki listened with interest, asking questions and falling silent when Judd told her about the plague of horsemen and the jailer who had killed Nada.

"Did you love her?"

Judd hesitated. "I'm not sure. I'd be lying
to say I wasn't interested in her. She was an
incredible person." He pulled a tattered piece
of paper from his wallet and handed it to
Vicki. "She wrote this, and her mother gave it
to me after she died."

Vicki opened the paper and spread it out
on her leg.

> *Dear Judd,*
> *My mother suggested I write this down
> so I won't forget. Maybe the GC is going
> to execute us, and if that happens, you can
> take comfort in the fact that I'm in a better
> place. Being with Christ is what our lives
> are all about. If they've killed me, I'm
> there, so don't be sad for me. I love you very
> much. From the moment you came to our
> family, I felt close to you. You were like a
> brother to me. Then, as my feelings grew
> deeper, you were more than that.*
>
> *But I have to tell you something. I feel
> it's only fair that I express this. As close as
> we became, in our talks and the time we
> spent together, I always felt there was some-
> thing missing. I couldn't put my finger on
> it until we came back to Israel and you
> backed away. I feel what I'm about to say
> is something that God wants me to say.*
>
> *I have prayed many nights about this.*

I've asked God to show me why I'm feeling this way. Honestly, I think something is holding you back. At first, I thought it was God. You're so sold out on him, and you want to live for him. But the more I thought and prayed, it became clear that God wasn't coming between us. I really believe there is someone else. You've never talked much about your friends in the States, but I sense there is someone there you care about deeply.

Maybe I'm making this up. If so, I apologize. But if I'm right and you find this letter, go back to her. You're a wonderful person with so much to offer. I have loved being your friend. I'm sorry for the trouble I caused you in New Babylon. I'm sorry for being difficult at times. (You had your moments too.) I'll look forward to seeing you again, whether it's in this life or the next. May God bless you.

Love,
Nada

Vicki's hands shook as she gingerly folded the page. "I can't believe that. She knew you well."

They talked more about Nada and her sacrifice as they returned to the main cabin. The sun had gone down, and Judd wanted to be sure to honor Zeke's request that they return before dark.

"Let me ask you something," Judd said. "Remember when I called and you were out with that guy in Iowa?"

Vicki nodded. "His name was Chad Harris. He actually showed up here a little while after you made it to Ohio." Vicki told Judd what Chad had done and how the GC had caught and executed him.

Judd couldn't believe it. "You obviously didn't want to hurt his feelings, but you didn't feel the same way about him as he felt about you?"

"Right. I felt really bad about it for weeks."

When they reached the main cabin, everyone had gathered around the computer for the latest from the Global Community News Network. The reporters showed more death and devastation throughout the world. Famous sites around the world that had survived the wrath of the Lamb earthquake were burning. The GC had tried to adapt, but it was clear this plague had paralyzed the enemies of God.

"In the United North American States, one man has risen to the challenge of the killer fires," the reporter said.

A face flashed on the screen, and Vicki groaned. "Fulcire," she said under her breath.

"Commander Kruno Fulcire says he won't let this latest natural disaster keep him from his duty," the reporter said.

"I've pledged my life to the ideals of the Global Community," Fulcire said from some darkened GC bunker. "My main mission over these past few months and years has been to ferret out rebels and punish them. I'm sticking with that mission, and we're offering even more money to any citizen brave and resourceful enough to bring in rebels during this time."

"How can people do that with all the fires?" the reporter said.

"Hunt them at night. We're watching radar and surveillance cameras for any movement and tracking down that movement when the heat allows. We may find more rebels now than at any other time."

"So there's truth to the rumors that the rebels, at least some of them, are immune to this wave of heat?"

Fulcire shifted in his chair. "I'm not saying that we know exactly who or what is out there during the day. I don't want to give the rebels any more credit than they deserve, but if they're foolish enough to go out in the fire and survive, we'll find a way to catch them."

Marshall Jameson smiled. "Sounds like they're trying to bluff us into staying put."

"Which is another good reason to go on the offensive," Judd said.

They watched the coverage a few more minutes. Then Colin Dial called for everyone's attention. "Before we sample some of Josey's desserts, I'd like to propose a toast." He held up a glass of juice, and the others grabbed full glasses from the table. "To Judd and Lionel, for surviving the long journey home."

Lionel held up his glass. "If I could add to that?"

Colin nodded.

"For the prayers of our friends. God answered in ways we couldn't have imagined, and we thank you."

"I might as well give mine and not let you two hog the spotlight," Zeke said. The others laughed. "To all the people we've known who believed and are no longer with us. And to my dad." He looked at the ceiling and gave a short salute. "I hope I can live long enough to make you proud."

Judd looked around to see if anyone else would add a toast. Charlie stepped forward. "I have one. To Judd and Vicki."

"To Judd and Vicki," everyone said.

Judd couldn't remember the last time he had eaten homemade cake. He devoured his first piece and went for seconds. The warmth of the group, the laughter and happy faces, were the perfect end to the evening. Though they had all experienced loss and the world was winding down like a huge clock, it felt good to have fun again.

Before the group went to their cabins, Marshall gave final instructions. "We're awaiting word from the Tribulation Force about the movement of supplies and people. Everybody be ready to help or welcome additions if we need to."

After an emotional time in prayer, everyone moved to their cabins. Judd lingered, talking to Conrad and Mark about the possibility of joining the Tribulation Force to move supplies.

Vicki talked with Becky Dial and others about Judd's return. As everyone filed out, Vicki touched Judd on the shoulder to say good night, but he excused himself and walked her to her cabin. The air was cool compared to the daytime temperature, and Vicki rubbed her arms.

"Great night, wasn't it?" Judd said.

"The best I can remember."

"I have something to apologize for."

"What?"

"Your birthday."

Vicki chuckled. "The whole world is burning, and you're worried about my birthday?"

"I had it written down to send you a message on your birthday, but we switched computers and it slipped my mind. When I finally remembered, it seemed kind of lame to just apologize, and I couldn't send this."

Judd pulled out a small package and Vicki gasped.

"I ran short on wrapping paper," Judd said.

Vicki unwrapped the newspaper and opened the box slowly. Shelly peeked out the cabin door, then closed it. Vicki heard snickers from inside, and Judd blushed.

"When we moved from Indiana to Ohio, we met a doctor who treated Lionel's arm. His wife had disappeared in the Rapture, and he'd kept this ever since he found it on her pillow."

Inside the box was a beautiful gold chain with a heart-shaped pendant. A diamond sparkled in the middle. Judd turned the heart around and pointed at elegant writing on the back that said *Ich Liebe Dich*.

"What's that mean?"

"The doctor said it's German for 'I love you.' He had studied in Germany and brought that back as an engagement gift for his wife. When I told him our story, he wanted me to give it to you." Judd took the necklace from the box and fastened it around Vicki's neck.

"I love it. And I'm glad you waited to give it to me." She gave Judd a hug.

He smiled and squeezed her hand. "See you at breakfast?"

"Wouldn't miss it."

TEN

Working for the Co-op

THE FIRST night was the hardest for Lionel. He told Marshall he would take the first watch for any GC activity, and when Marshall protested, Lionel put his hand on the man's arm. "It would do me good to stay up. I'm not doing too well with all the changes."

Zeke volunteered to stay at the computer with Lionel, and they had a good talk. "Must be kind of hard for you with all the excitement over Judd and Vicki."

"I expected it," Lionel said. "I don't know which was harder, running from the GC these last few years or keeping up with Judd's love life."

Zeke smiled. "You've seen a lot more of the inner workings of the GC than any of us here."

"And I've seen a lot of death." Lionel told

Zeke about Conrad's brother, Taylor
Graham, and how he had died. Zeke asked
about Pavel, their young friend who had
invited them to New Babylon, who had also
died. When Lionel got to the stories of Nada
and her brother, Kasim, he shook his head.
"I think we need to change the subject."

"Good idea. Tell me what God's done with
you since you left."

Lionel held up the stump of his left arm.
"He did this."

"Are you upset about it?"

"No. I just don't understand why it had to
happen."

"Accidents happen."

Lionel nodded. "I guess that's one thing
that changed while I was away. Before the
Rapture, I thought about God in terms of him
being way out there and us down here trying
to do stuff for him. When I became a true
believer, I realized he wanted to be with us,
helping us. But I still thought living for God
meant doing stuff for him, trying to convince
people he's there and he loves them. All the
pressure was on me to perform, you know? If
somebody didn't become a believer, I felt
responsible, like it was my fault."

"And that's changed?"

"Big time. I know I need to reach out as
much as I can, but the past few years have

taught me this is God's battle. He's the one drawing people to himself and fighting the enemy. If I talk with someone and they don't become a believer, I feel sad, but I don't feel guilty. God really is in control."

Zeke nodded. "That's a hard lesson to learn. We want to keep control of things and make it all about us when this is all about God." He paused. "But how does that affect your arm? If God's in control, he let it happen."

Lionel stared at the computer screen. "Sometimes at night I'll reach out for a drink of water or rub my eyes, and I'll realize I'm still reaching with my left hand. And then I'll have nightmares about the rest of my arm under that rock."

"Ever have any pain in the arm that's gone?"

"You bet. It shoots up and down the tendons and into my fingers . . . fingers that aren't even there."

"They call that phantom pain, but it's supposed to be just as real as if your arm were still there."

"I thought it would go away, but it hasn't."

"Give it time," Zeke said. "I watched you tonight during the celebration. You've adjusted well to the physical part, eating with one hand and everything else. But there's a mental side to this, an emotional thing you have to adjust to. I can't say I can help much, but if you need somebody to talk to . . ."

"Thanks," Lionel said.

"And there's something I've been workin' on since I heard about the accident." Zeke walked to a storage closet and pulled out a box. He laid it at Lionel's feet.

Lionel gasped when he opened the lid. Inside was a plastic replica of the lower portion of his arm. "How did you—"

"As soon as I heard what happened, I went looking on the Internet and through our sources at the Co-op for what they call prosthetic devices. Then I realized I had most of the materials right here, so I went to work. The hard part was making a mold for the plastic. I must have tried a dozen times before it came out right. Go ahead—try it out."

Lionel lifted the gadget into place. It fit perfectly against the end of his arm.

Zeke helped him fasten it. "You ain't gonna be lifting with it or using two pistols to fight the GC, but it does move with pressure." He showed Lionel how to turn his hand and move the lower arm by shifting his weight.

"It's perfect," Lionel said, holding out his new left hand. "Put her there."

Zeke shook Lionel's left hand and smiled. "I don't know why God allowed that to happen either, but I wouldn't doubt it if he was preparing you for something."

"He's going to have to hurry if he wants to use me," Lionel said. "There's only a year left before Jesus comes back."

Vicki liked the fact that Judd hadn't kissed her good night. The slower they took this, the better, as far as she was concerned. As she lay in bed, she held the golden heart up to the moonlight streaming in the window and watched the reflection dance against the ceiling. Shelly and Janie had moved into the room with her and had gushed over the present.

"It's so romantic!" Janie had said.

"Is that an engagement necklace?" Shelly said.

Vicki grinned. "The reports of our wedding have been greatly exaggerated."

Now, as the others slept, Vicki wondered what would happen. She had been waiting for so long she didn't know how to act now that Judd was actually here. She closed her eyes and thought of a scene from a movie where two people had been married in a secret ceremony. She drifted off to sleep clutching the golden heart.

Over the next few days, Judd tried to help out
with whatever jobs needed to be done at the
campground. The latest news from the Co-op
suggested they would need to make room for
a group that had been hiding south of Chicago, where the GC were more active.

"It's easier to move people than supplies,"
Rayford Steele had said, "and this will get our
people out of harm's way."

Judd kept in contact with Sam Goldberg
for the latest in Petra. The boy continued his
Petra Diaries, and each new writing was filled
with facts and observations about Tsion's
and Chaim's messages.

Judd also spoke with Chang Wong in New
Babylon and encouraged him to use the heat
wave to escape Nicolae Carpathia and the
palace. Chang resisted, saying the Tribulation
Force needed him there now more than ever.

"There's so much to move—equipment,
aircraft, food, and other supplies," Chang
said. "If I can hang on long enough, we'll all
be in a lot better shape for the final year."

"What's it like there?" Judd said.

"Everyone is obsessed with finding shelter
from the sun. The first couple of days were
the worst. People went underground and set
up their offices and living quarters. They

work at night and try to sleep during the day, but some don't even want to go out at night because of all the bodies and burned-out vehicles."

"What about Carpathia? I hope he's mad about all this."

"He says the heat's not bothering him at all."

"You're kidding."

"No, the sun comes through the glass ceiling and roasts the whole floor. His secretary is underground, but Nicolae orders people around all day from his office."

"Can anyone work in the palace?"

"On the lower floors, they've painted the windows black to keep out the sun, and some can work there. The weirdest thing happened the other day after Nicolae told his secretary he was going into the courtyard to sunbathe."

Judd shook his head. "And I suppose he did it."

"I snuck to a corner window and scraped a hole in the black coating. Carpathia took off his shirt and lay on a concrete bench and soaked in the rays."

"How long did he stay there?"

"He was out there at least an hour. Flames were licking at the concrete and all around him. I listened to a recording of Leon Fortunato with their head security guy, Akbar. Leon said he couldn't stand within twenty feet of Nicolae after the sunbathing incident because it was too hot."

"We should start calling him Nicolae the blowtorch."

Chang laughed. "Leon said Nicolae's shoes smoked. There were sparks in his hair. Even the buttons of his suit had melted."

"It just shows he's not really human."

"You won't believe what happened after that," Chang continued. "I listened in to a conversation between Smoky Shoes and Technical Services. He wanted a telescope set up so he could look directly at the sun at noon."

"What could he possibly want that for?"

"He said he wanted to record whether the sun has grown and if bursts of flame from its surface would be visible."

"Don't tell me he actually did it."

"I watched him. He looked at the sun for several minutes. He left, and when he came back the telescope had melted. That night he told the technician he had seen the flares dancing on the sun's surface. The techie laughed, thinking it was a joke, and Carpathia turned mean."

"What did he say?"

"He said, 'The sun, moon, and stars bow to me.' "

Judd felt a chill. He knew Carpathia was the Antichrist, but he was more than that now. Since Nicolae had risen from the dead, Dr. Ben-Judah and others believed that the man was literally indwelt by Satan. God's enemy would be defeated, but not before he did everything he could to hurt God's people. Satan, as Jesus had said, was a liar and a murderer from the beginning. He would use all his weapons to try to block God's plan.

"Carpathia has to know his time is running out," Judd said.

"Don't think the guy will ever think logically. He's trying to convince everyone around him that he's still king of the world."

"Even though everybody's burning up? Chang, this is the perfect time for you to get away. Think of what they'll do to you if they find out who you really serve."

"There's still too much to do with the Tribulation Force. Besides, nobody suspects me."

"Just don't make any mistakes. The first could be your last."

Vicki was pleased with the progress they were making with the cabins. Clemson Stoddard turned out to be a great carpenter. When he wasn't helping repair old cabins or construct new ones, he was reading Tsion Ben-Judah's Web site or sitting in on classes Vicki and the others offered newer believers.

Clemson had gone from looking like a hermit to being neatly dressed. He was always polite, and he had as many questions as anyone about the end of the world and what was going to happen next.

Vicki was answering one of his questions by drawing a time line of the Tribulation when she turned and noticed Judd had slipped into the back. She continued, trying to keep her focus on the class.

Marshall called everyone to dinner, and Judd walked with her to the main cabin.

"Don't do that again," Vicki said.

"Do what?"

"It makes me nervous when you're back there."

Judd stopped her and turned to face her. "You are one of the best teachers I've ever seen. I was only in there a few minutes, but the way you explained the time line was incredible."

Vicki blushed and rolled her eyes.

"I mean it. You don't know how proud I was when we were in Israel and you showed up on the video screen above the stadium."

"Bet you were surprised too."

"You bet and a little bit scared for you. But when 'Vicki B.' started talking about God and telling people how to become a believer, I was in awe."

"So you didn't think I could do that kind of thing?"

"I didn't take the time to think about anybody else back then. But it's clear now that God had something more planned for you, and if I hadn't gotten out of the way, it might never have happened."

Vicki smiled. "Care to escort the teacher to dinner?"

"I'd be honored."

As the sun went down, Judd and Vicki met with Marshall and Zeke. Judd was excited because he knew Marshall had had a phone meeting scheduled with Rayford Steele earlier in the day.

"The Trib Force heard from the group you stayed with in the library, but they haven't been able to get back in touch with them," Marshall said. "They're wondering if you could meet them and help lead them to those people."

"I'm there," Judd said.

"Before you agree, you have to understand that we don't have any idea when this plague will lift. You could be in the air when it gets cool, and the GC could converge on you."

Judd bit his lip. "In that case, I have one request."

"What's that?" Marshall said.

"That Vicki goes with me."

ELEVEN

Library Mission

As soon as the sun came up two days later, Judd drove Vicki south in the Humvee to meet a Tribulation Force plane. The small airport lay in ruins, skeletons of planes smoldering under the wrecked hangar. The runway was still in good shape though, and it wasn't long after they arrived that the plane touched down.

Judd had hoped Rayford Steele would be aboard or perhaps another of the higher ranking Trib Force members. Instead, the door opened and Westin Jakes appeared. Judd introduced Vicki, and Westin shook hands with her. "So you're the reason Judd was so eager to get back to the States."

Vicki smiled. "And you're one of the reasons he made it back in one piece."

"Have a seat. We'll get in the air, and I'll explain our mission."

"This is an awfully big plane for the three of us," Judd said.

"Hopefully on the way back we'll have the thing full of your friends from that library," Westin said. He asked Judd the specific location of the library, and Judd told him.

Westin went to the back of the plane as Judd buckled in behind the pilot's seat. He told Vicki more about what Westin had been through and the episode in Paris.

"If Judd and Lionel hadn't been there to help, my head would be in some bread basket in France right now," Westin said when he returned to the cockpit. "I heard about Lionel's arm. Tell him I've been praying for him."

"He'll appreciate that," Judd said. "Have you heard anything about Z-Van lately?"

Westin smiled. "You didn't hear about the concert a few days ago?" He held up a hand, taxied the runway, and got them airborne.

When it was safe, he put the plane on autopilot and turned. "Z-Van was doing his pro-Carpathia show, I guess trying to make people think there's really nothing wrong with the world, when it starts getting hot onstage."

"This was the day the heat wave started?" Vicki said.

Westin nodded.

"And you were there?" Judd said.

"I was delivering supplies to a group of believers near the event. It was a night job, real secret kind of stuff. I had dropped the supplies off and was heading back to the plane when I found out about Z-Van's appearance. I couldn't help myself."

"Don't tell me you showed up at the concert!" Judd said.

"I kept a good distance. I was wearing my fake GC outfit, so nobody paid much attention. Normally Z-Van doesn't perform in the daytime, at least he didn't while I was with him. But the GC must have convinced him to do this late-morning gig."

"I don't guess they needed a warm-up band." Judd laughed.

"Good one," Westin said. "I noticed people in the crowd were getting restless way before show time. They were wiping their faces and shielding their eyes from the sun. Some held blankets or umbrellas over them. Well, the music started and Z-Van came out, but people were getting so hot that they couldn't pay attention."

"And you probably had no idea what was going on," Judd said.

"Right. I was a little warm, but these people were going crazy. Z-Van runs out expecting some kind of ovation, and there are nothing but screams. He reaches for the microphone and then drops it on the ground like he's picked up a poisonous snake. That's when I noticed something funny about the video screen onstage. Images of Nicolae and Leon Fortunato were flashing when all of a sudden the screen started rippling. Then a big brown spot appeared in the middle, and it burst into flames."

"I'll bet that got Z-Van's attention," Judd said.

"He was still trying to pick up the microphone, but the thing had melted. He pried it up with a drumstick, but it was fried."

"What did the crowd do?" Vicki said.

"Everybody panicked. It was as if the heat just descended like a swarm of bees, and they ran for cover. Problem was, they ran over each other. Hundreds were killed from being trampled before the first person ever caught fire."

"How awful!" Vicki said.

"One of those miracle workers came onstage and tried to calm the crowd. He was wearing a long, black robe and had a lapel microphone on. The speakers started crackling and popping like something was wrong with the lines, but when I looked closer, it was the miracle guy with flames licking at his outfit. He ran screaming to the back with the rest of the band members."

"You think Z-Van survived?" Judd said.

"The GC hasn't said he's dead, but they also didn't report anything about the concert. There must have been thousands on the ground, their bodies just piles of ashes. The stage, lights, all their instruments—everything went up in smoke."

As they flew, Westin told them the other things he had experienced while flying for the Co-op. Judd was amazed at all God had accomplished through this man he and Lionel had reached out to.

When they neared their destination, Westin outlined the plan for the group at the library. He handed Judd a printout of a message the Tribulation Force had received two days earlier.

> *Dear Captain Steele or anyone else in the Tribulation Force,*
>
> *A young man named Judd Thompson gave us this address and told us if we felt in danger in any way we should contact you. The power has been spotty in our area, but there have been sightings of GC near us at night. If you could please get back to us with an escape plan, we would be grateful. I don't feel I should give you our location in case this gets intercepted by the GC. Below*

you'll see Judd's e-mail, and he can tell you where to find us.

The group signed the note, "Waiting in the stacks." Judd thought of the people he had met at the library. "How are we going to get from wherever you'll land to the library?"

"Good question. You'll have to ask God that one. We have people praying about the transportation question right now."

Westin used his phone to call San Diego and confirm the nearest landing strip that could handle their large airplane. "I was right. The nearest strip is about twenty miles from your friends." He glanced at his watch. "If everything goes as planned, we can get back to Wisconsin with a couple hours to spare and have your friends at the camp meet you with another vehicle."

"What if we don't get back before sundown?" Vicki said.

"That's why we have people praying," Westin said.

As they flew close to the ground, Vicki looked out the window at plumes of smoke rising from buildings. There were no other planes in sight, which was an eerie feeling.

The earth looked like a shell that had been used and thrown away. The most drastic change had come with the wrath of the Lamb earthquake, but even with that, the GC leaders had found a way to bounce back and restore services. With this plague of heat, the earth had come to a standstill during daylight hours. It was an advantage Vicki had never dreamed of for believers, but she couldn't help feeling sad for the poor people who had chosen Carpathia.

Westin told her and Judd that the Tribulation Force members were free to come and go as long as they were careful to plan their travel into time zones that kept them in daylight as long as possible. There was news that the polar ice caps were melting faster than at any time in history, and huge weather systems threatened the coasts on every continent. Many coastlines were already buried under massive floods.

"What are you doing after this assignment?" Vicki said.

"We're trying to coordinate our planes and storehouses. Chang Wong in New Babylon has it all graphed out. If this heat wave continues, we'll have enough food and supplies for believers for at least a year. That's what we hope."

The plane touched down on a runway so short Vicki thought they were going to run off the end. Westin led them off the plane and secured the door, though there was no reason to think anyone would get to it before they returned.

When they were on the ground, Vicki saw the devastation of a more populated city for the first time. What appeared to be million-dollar homes looked like the remains of old campfires. Fencing around the airport had melted from the intense heat.

Vicki noticed a creepy silence. In the woods she had sensed the lack of animals during the day, but here, where there should have been traffic and honking and buses, the only sound was the occasional collapse of a building or the crackling of fires.

"Follow me," Westin said. He led them to a concrete parking garage. "We haven't used this airfield as a base of operations, but I'm willing to bet there's a vehicle—" He paused, staring into the distance. "Would you look at that?"

Vicki glanced to her right at a small bus sitting in front of what was left of the main terminal building. It looked like the kind of bus used to transport disabled children. She was shocked that in the midst of the heat, the vehicle hadn't caught fire.

"Is this your answer to prayer?" Judd said as they ran to the bus.

"Works for me," Westin said.

They climbed in and Westin chuckled. "Even has a full tank of gas."

Though they had found transportation quickly, finding the library proved to be more difficult. It was nearly 3:30 local time when they finally pulled close to the structure. Judd said he had worried that the building wouldn't be there, but it still stood.

Vicki was glad to retrace some of Judd's steps. She had heard about the library and pictured it in her mind, but seeing it in person made her feel more a part of his story.

Judd opened the front door and called for his friends. There was no answer. "They're probably downstairs. Come on."

Judd took the stairs two at a time and bounded through the lower floor of the darkened library. He flipped on the light switch, but nothing happened.

"They said they were having power problems," Westin said.

Vicki was immediately hit by the smell of old books. She hadn't spent that much time in the library as a kid, but the times when she had to do a research project or look up something on the Internet had been fun.

Each time she walked through her library in Mount Prospect, she wondered why she didn't read more.

Westin snagged Judd's shirt and pulled him back toward the stairwell. "Something's not right."

"There can't be GC here," Judd said. "The building would have—"

Someone moaned from behind the stacks of books. Vicki was startled when she heard pounding on the window upstairs. The three moved back up the steps cautiously, and Vicki gasped when she saw a face at the window.

Judd hit the front door and rushed outside.

Judd grabbed the leader of the group's hands and shook furiously. He introduced Vicki and Westin while the man caught his breath.

"Two nights ago . . . the GC came . . . we only had a few seconds to get out the back," the man gasped.

"Where is everyone?" Judd said.

"Scattered. Some of us have hidden in a burned-out building a few blocks away. We prayed you'd come."

"And there are Peacekeepers hiding downstairs in the library?"

"Some are just citizens, but others are officers. I think they have guns."

"I don't get it," Vicki said. "If everybody in there is loyal to Carpathia, why hasn't the building burned?"

Westin pursed his lips. "Let's get the rest of your group and get out of here."

The man led them to three separate sites and gathered more than twenty people into the bus. All were overjoyed to see Judd, glad they wouldn't have to spend another night hiding. One of the last to be picked up was a woman in her forties who scanned the bus and turned to Westin. "We can't leave yet. Howard's not here."

"Who's Howard?" Judd said.

"My son. You probably met him when you were here."

"I remember a young guy who argued—"

The woman nodded. "That's him. I don't know if he made it out of the library. I haven't seen him since that night."

"Where else could he be?" Judd said.

"Wait a minute," Vicki said. "If the library is still standing, maybe Howard's hiding there."

Westin looked at his watch. "Listen, people, we're running out of time. If we don't get in the air soon—"

"We have to try," Vicki said, glancing at Judd. "If the GC find him tonight—"

"Who's to say they haven't already found him and chopped off his head?" a man behind them said.

Howard's mother put a hand to her mouth and started crying.

"Don't worry," Vicki said. She looked at Judd. "We are going to try, right?"

Judd motioned for Westin to move outside, and the man followed. "I can't pull rank on you because I don't have any, but I'd like to go back and see if this kid is inside the library. Vicki's got a hunch, and usually she's right."

"Don't let your judgment get clouded," Westin said. "If we get caught out after dark, we could jeopardize the whole Tribulation Force. If we're in the air, the GC could launch a missile or track us with radar."

Judd looked at his watch. "Let us go to the library, and you head to the plane. If we're not there in an hour, leave."

"I can't do that. And you know if Captain Steel or anybody else hears about this, you won't go on another mission."

Judd looked at Vicki, who had her arm draped around Howard's mother. He jumped back inside the bus and called for quiet. "Does anyone know of a vehicle near here?"

An older man raised a hand. "I have an old Beetle in a garage a couple of blocks that way. It was still there yesterday when I checked."

"Where are the keys?" Judd said.

The man fished in his pocket and threw them at Judd. "Go left at that stop sign, and then two blocks. It's the only garage still standing."

"You can't do this," Westin said as Judd raced down the stairs.

Judd turned. "One hour. We'll meet you at the airstrip." He looked at the distraught woman. "And don't worry, ma'am. If your son's there, we'll find him."

"Bless you," she said.

The air brakes sounded behind them while Judd and Vicki hurried toward the garage.

"You think we can make it in an hour?" Vicki said.

"If we don't, it's going to be a long night."

TWELVE

Rescue

THE CAR sputtered and coughed when Judd turned the key. The Volkswagen wasn't just old—it was ancient, with rust spots on the body, balding tires, and an inch of dust. Vicki coughed as she jumped in the passenger seat. Judd tried to start the engine again, but it wheezed and shook.

"Maybe we should walk to the library," Vicki said.

"We'll never make it back to the airport in time," Judd said, pumping the gas pedal. He turned the ignition again, and blue smoke poured from the exhaust pipe. He revved the engine, put the car in reverse, and backed out.

The car chugged and clunked its way through the smoky streets, leaving a trail of smoke of its own. Judd glanced at Vicki and smiled. "You think the GC will stop us for polluting the air?"

Vicki gritted her teeth. "You're doing this for me, aren't you?"

"In a way, but I'm doing it for Howard and his mother too."

"I saw Westin's face. If we don't get back to that plane in time we're in big trouble, right?"

Judd made a sharp turn, and the tires squealed. "This is the right thing to do, and not just because it was your idea. We're going to find Howard and get to the plane. Besides, Westin owes me."

Judd parked on what had been the lawn of the library. All the grass had burned, along with the flowers and shrubbery that surrounded the building.

"How do you want to do this?" Vicki said.

"We don't have time for strategy," Judd said.

"If there are GC here and they have guns, they'll use them."

Judd scratched his chin. "Maybe we can make them think there are more than two of us."

"It doesn't matter how many they think we are—if they start shooting, we're in trouble."

Vicki already noticed a change in the way Judd handled things. In the old days, he would have simply rushed inside without talking with anyone. He might have dismissed the idea of coming back altogether. But something had changed, and it made Vicki want to follow him inside.

Judd stopped, picked up a huge rock, and pointed to the tinted glass below them. "That's the stairwell. Grab a rock and see if you can break that glass."

Judd's first throw glanced off and landed below. Vicki moved for a better angle and heaved a chunk of concrete. The glass crashed and fell inside the stairwell.

"Good job," Judd said, picking up another stone. A minute later the stairwell was filled with glass, and the sun reached the fire doors below.

Judd climbed down the small hill and carefully crawled through one of the broken windows. He reached back to help Vicki through, then propped open the fire doors with two rocks. Immediately Vicki heard voices whispering inside. A woman was crying, and someone tried to shush her.

Vicki moved into the basement and

thought about the GC's perspective. They were trying to stay out of the fire, and here were people walking through it as though it was nothing. "They must be terrified," she whispered.

Judd pointed to the opposite end of the building. "I saw two windows down on that end. There must be an office or something. The more light we can get in here, the better."

Vicki nodded, grabbed two rocks, and hurried in the shadows to the other end of the room. Judd was right. A sign on a door at the end said *Library Director*. Vicki tried the doorknob, and to her surprise the door opened. She hurled stones at the window behind the desk, and the glass shattered, letting in some of the deadly heat.

Another crash on the other side of the library and a shaft of light lit the room. Judd walked into the light.

"What do you want with us?" a man yelled, his voice full of fear.

"Why are you trying to kill us?" a woman sobbed.

Vicki froze and strained to see the people. "It's getting really hot," someone said.

"We don't want to hurt you," Judd said. Vicki had never heard this voice of Judd's. It was full of authority, though he wasn't yelling. "Throw out your weapons, and we'll get what we need and leave."

"Don't do it," someone whispered. "It's a trick."

"That blacked-out window behind you will come down if you don't slide your weapons out now."

Vicki held her breath.

Several guns clattered on the floor. Judd gathered them up cautiously and returned to the shadows. "All right, step forward and come to the front of the stacks."

"He's going to shoot us!" a woman said.

"You won't be harmed. Step forward."

"The sun's too hot," a man said.

Judd kicked the rocks from the stair doors and let them close. The room darkened, and several people stepped forward. "Sit," Judd said.

Vicki counted twelve people, four of them wearing Global Community uniforms. They sat in front of the bookshelves, sweating and breathing heavily, eyes darting from Judd to Vicki.

"Is this all of you?" Judd said.

"It's everybody," an officer said.

Judd placed the guns on the floor and squatted. "How did you find this place?"

The officer laughed. "What do you mean?

It's the only building standing for blocks. We ran in here to escape the heat. More come every night."

"Did you see anyone in here when you came?"

"Nobody," the officer said.

"I thought I saw some Judah-ites run out," a younger woman said. "They ran into the sunlight just like . . ."

"Just like what?"

She hesitated. "Just like you."

As Judd spoke with the group, Vicki wandered down the corridor, looking for a hiding place. She noticed movement in one of the locked study rooms along the north wall. A series of doors opened on small, five-by-five-foot rooms. Vicki got on all fours and crept toward the door at the end. She stood and looked through the window. A young man with the mark of the believer on his forehead moved behind a desk. He was startled when Vicki knocked on the door.

"Howard?" Vicki said.

The young man's mouth opened in shock. "How did you know my name?"

"Get out of there. We don't have much time."

Howard was thin and no taller than Vicki, with a slight beard. His clothes were tight, and his hair stuck up in the back.

"I've been waiting two days for someone to come get me," Howard said as he snatched his backpack and followed Vicki. "Do you know where my mom and—"

Vicki put a finger to her lips. "Keep quiet until we get out of here." She led Howard to the stairwell door and cleared her throat. "I have him."

Judd grabbed the guns from the floor and stood.

"I thought you said we could have our guns back," the officer said.

"You don't need guns to survive this plague by God."

"You *are* Judah-ites," a woman said.

A gun clicked from the back of the library, and Vicki ducked as the wood above her head splintered. Automatic weapon fire filled the room, and Judd hit the stairwell doors hard, spreading light onto the people sitting in front of the stacks. All of them screamed and ran for the darkness as Judd, Vicki, and Howard bolted upstairs.

"Get in the car!" Judd yelled as they jumped over the broken glass on the stairway. More gunfire erupted, but the shooter quickly ran out of ammunition.

While Judd plopped the weapons in the

backseat, Howard jumped inside. "Where are you taking me?"

"Hang on," Judd said, firing up the Beetle. "We're headed for the airport."

The car's tires spun on the lawn when Judd pulled away. Vicki looked back to make sure no one was following them and noticed more smoke. Judd slowed long enough to see the roof of the library begin to curl. Windows on the upper floor of the building shattered, and smoke billowed. Vicki put her window down a little, then rolled it up when she heard people inside screaming.

Judd had clicked his stopwatch as soon as Westin and the others in the bus pulled away. He looked at it now and shook his head. They had less than twenty minutes to make it to the airport before the hour was up.

He flew through the streets, made a wrong turn, backtracked, then headed in the right direction.

"How'd you guys know I was there?" Howard said.

"Your mom noticed you were missing," Vicki said. "What happened?"

"Our leader told us to stay together, but I

got fed up with all the rules. I went into one of those study rooms, and when I woke up the GC had moved in. I tried to slip out last night, but I got scared."

"You should have listened to your leader," Judd said.

Howard rolled his eyes. "Thanks."

Judd dialed Westin, but the call didn't go through.

"A lot of the big towers are down," Howard said. "I heard that before the power went out."

By the time they made it to the airport, Judd's watch showed the trip had taken an hour and a half. He jammed the keys in his pocket, slammed the door of the Beetle, and joined Vicki outside. The sun was fading, and they had only an hour of daylight left.

"Don't be too hard on Howard," Vicki whispered. "Westin will be back for us tomorrow, right?"

Judd sighed. "I hope so, but you know if he talks to anyone in the Trib Force they'll blacklist us."

Vicki shrugged. "Well, that'll just give us more time together."

Howard got out of the car and approached them with his hands in his pockets. "I'm sorry. I didn't mean to cause you trouble. Guess I've really messed things up."

Judd put a hand on Howard's shoulder. "Everybody makes mistakes. I just hope you live long enough to learn from them."

"We need to find a place to hide, right?" Howard said. "I think I might know the spot."

Howard pointed to the parking garage, and Judd parked the car behind some burned-out vehicles. They wound their way through the stairwell, made it to the roof, and found a spot by the door.

"I'm hungry," Vicki said.

Howard opened his backpack and pulled out a couple of sandwiches and some candy bars. "I had these stashed away in my little corner so I wouldn't have to go out and eat with the others." He gave the food to Vicki, and she divided it equally among them. Judd rushed into the terminal and came back a few minutes later with several bottles of water he had found in an employee kitchen.

"What do we do if the GC come tonight?" Howard said.

"The only people who knew about you are part of the ashes of that library," Judd said.

"What if somebody heard the plane?"

Judd shrugged, and Vicki huddled close to him as the sun finally went down. Judd tried calling Westin, but the connection didn't ring. He thought about calling the group in Wisconsin but decided against it. They were on their own for the night.

Vicki suggested they pray, and the three bowed their heads. Judd and Vicki prayed freely and paused to let Howard join.

After a few seconds he took a breath and struggled through a brief prayer. "God, I want to thank you for these people who helped me. If the GC had caught me back there, I don't know what would have happened. I ask you to forgive me for being so . . . hardheaded and help Judd and Vicki make it back to their friends."

THIRTEEN

The Longest Night

JUDD was surprised at how fast the temperature dropped after the sun went down. Vicki snuggled close, and the two tried to stay warm. Though fires burned throughout the city, they feared building one on the roof would draw attention.

In the daytime, the only sounds Judd had heard, other than their car and plane, were the crackling fires and the whistling of the wind. At night, however, the city seemed to come alive. Dogs barked, motorcycles whined, and people shouted in the distance. But the worst sound was the cries of people who had lost family and friends. The high-pitched wails of men and women in pain echoed through the smoldering ruins.

"I feel so bad for them," Vicki whispered. "If they'd chosen God instead of Carpathia, they wouldn't be hurting."

Judd looked at Howard, who was looking out at the city over the concrete wall. "How long have you lived here?"

"All my life. I never thought I'd see anything like this."

"Tell us your story," Vicki said.

"You don't want to know about me."

"Come on," Judd said.

Howard sighed, turned, and slid to a sitting position. "My dad left when I was four or five. My mom did her best, but by the time I was a teenager, I didn't want anybody running my life. She worked two jobs, so she was out till all hours of the night.

"I hung out with a bunch of friends, and a lot of times I didn't even show up for school. We'd party all night, which meant we'd buy some beer—we didn't have much money for drugs. I guess you could say I was wasted. I was just kind of out there."

"You didn't know any Christians?" Vicki said.

Howard laughed. "I saw them on TV, you know, the evangelists and all. Preachers who wanted me to send money. I knew kids whose parents dragged them to church, but they pretty much did the same stuff I did.

"But there was this one kid, Kirk. He was just as wild as we were, only not in the same way."

"What do you mean?" Vicki said.

"He could do stuff on a skateboard you wouldn't believe. No helmet. No fear. He was skinny, like me, with a pointy nose. He kind of looked like a bird, come to think of it. His hair was always sticking up in the back, and his body was always moving. You know, even if he was standing still he was moving, cracking his knuckles, crossing his legs, snapping his neck. You just couldn't stop the guy."

"What happened to him?" Vicki said.

"We were hanging out one night when Kirk came by. He was riding a new scooter he'd saved up for. His dad didn't like him riding at night, but he had to show it off. You should have seen his face when he pulled up. You would have thought he had a Mercedes. He'd been talking about the thing for a whole year." Howard looked at the floor and pursed his lips.

"What?" Judd said. "Did you do something to him?"

"We made fun of it. We asked him why he threw away his money on a toy. Said it would probably only go ten miles an hour. I knew we hurt him. He just wanted to show it to us."

"When you get with a group, it's hard not to put others down," Vicki said.

"Yeah, well I never got the chance to tell him I was sorry."

"What happened?"

"He gunned the thing and drove down an alley, trying to show off. I told the other guys he was going to wipe out if he wasn't careful. He must have been going fifty when he came out the other side. We heard a squeal and a crash. And when we got there, a guy was standing by the scooter saying, 'He drove right out in front of me.' The impact had thrown Kirk about thirty feet into some garbage cans. He was still breathing when we got to him. The driver called an ambulance. Kirk wasn't wearing a helmet, and I'm not sure he had much of a chance, anyway."

"That must have been awful for you," Vicki said.

"Yeah. I went to the hospital, but I couldn't face his family. The next day I heard he'd died and that all of us were invited to the funeral."

"Did you go?" Judd said.

Howard nodded. "It was the first time I heard any kind of religion that made sense."

"What do you mean?" Vicki said.

"Kirk wasn't real religious, you know. He didn't push it on any of us. When we'd get beer or the occasional joint, he'd find some excuse to leave. He did smoke cigarettes, but

I could tell he felt bad about it and tried like everything to quit. He actually invited me and my mom to church a couple of times, but I always made some excuse.

"Anyway, the funeral was at his church, and you wouldn't believe all the people. There were church kids sitting next to stoners and freaks. Just about every group in school had known Kirk. We were there to say good-bye and try to deal with the loss, but the family had asked a guy to speak."

"Someone from the church?" Judd said.

"Yeah, a youth leader. He had kind of a high-pitched voice and was short, but what he said made all of us want to listen. He talked about Kirk and nailed him. I mean, the guy knew him inside and out. Even talked about Kirk's struggle to kick tobacco.

"Then he told us that we'd all known Kirk for a reason. He was quiet for a moment, and I could hear people sniffling. He said God had called us to a divine appointment that day to hear Kirk's biggest hope for each one of us.

"He pulled out a wrinkled piece of paper and put on his glasses. It was so quiet you could have heard a mouse burp. I looked at Kirk's mom and dad, and I don't think they even knew what the guy was going to say."

Howard stopped his story and turned his head. "You guys hear that?"

Judd stood up. He had been so engrossed in Howard's story that he had forgotten they were keeping an eye out for the Global Community.

"Maybe this wasn't the best place to hide," Vicki said.

Judd peeked over the railing and scanned the area. A black dog pawed at debris below them, and Judd sighed. "Keep going. I want to hear what happened."

"So the guy pulls out this paper and starts reading. I guess Kirk had asked a bunch of questions, and the youth guy had told him to write down his thoughts and dreams."

"What was on the paper?" Vicki said.

"Kirk started with something like, 'I don't understand why God could forgive me for the stuff I've done and not forgive the others.' You know, he just kind of went off on God and asked why all his friends seemed so unhappy and how Kirk felt guilty for not reaching out to them and helping them. That was the main thing the youth guy said, that Kirk came to him feeling guilty that he didn't have the courage to tell all of us about Jesus.

"That's when he read the prayer. I'll never forget it. 'God, I'm asking you to give me the courage to help all my friends hear about you.

I don't know how you're going to do it, but I ask you to work through me to tell them the truth.' That was it. The guy folded the paper and put it back in his pocket. He told us that God had worked it out to have all of us in one place so we could hear about Kirk's faith."

"What did he say then?" Judd said.

Howard bit his lip. "I remember him talking about Jesus and dying on the cross and wanting to forgive us, but I was so upset about being the reason Kirk was dead that I couldn't concentrate. I remember him saying that one day Jesus was going to come back for his followers and take them away. When the service was over, the youth guy asked people to come forward and give their lives to God. I slipped out the back door and went home."

"Did you ever talk with the youth leader?" Judd said.

"I was going to a couple of times but chickened out. I was also going to go see Kirk's parents and tell them how sorry I was, but I never got the chance."

"Why not?" Vicki said.

"They all disappeared about two weeks later. A lot of my friends I hung out with were gone. Some of the goths. A bunch of the drama kids. There wasn't a group that had been at that funeral that didn't lose somebody. There were all kinds of theories about what had happened—from space aliens to some kind of chemical reaction—but I knew as soon as I went back to school and saw all those people gone that it was supernatural. God had come back for his own, and I was left behind."

"What did you do?" Vicki said.

"I went back to the church. The youth guy had a bunch of Bibles and some stuff to read. I took a Bible and some of the papers and showed them to my mom. She was the first to pray, and then I did." Howard looked around the rooftop and pinched the bridge of his nose. "I know I haven't been a very good believer like you guys, but I really want to be."

"It's not about being good," Judd said. "If we all had to live perfectly after God forgave us, we'd be in deep trouble."

"But I've done just about everything I could to make my mom and the others who helped us miserable."

"God wants to change you from the inside out," Vicki said, "but you have to let him."

"I want that. . . ."

"Then tell him," Vicki said. "Pray right now and tell God you're giving him the rest of your life to use however he wants. Thank him for saving you and making you a

believer, and ask him to help you grow. He'll
do it. He really will."

Howard bowed his head, and Judd saw his
lips moving.

A siren wailed and all three jumped. They
crouched beneath the concrete wall and
listened as a GC squad car pulled into the
airport. The swirling lights cast eerie shadows
through the hovering smoke. When Judd
heard voices, he crawled to the edge and
peeked over. A uniformed GC officer spoke
with a man at the airport entrance. Their
voices carried across the parking lot.

"He came inside looking for something to
eat, I guess, but all he found was a few
bottles of water," the man said.

"And he walked back outside?"

"I think so. I wasn't about to follow into
the sunshine, but it didn't seem to bother
him."

"How long after the plane took off?" the
officer said.

"About a half hour. I heard a rattle and
bang, like he was driving an old Volkswagen.
You can't miss those engines, the way they
whistle and ping—"

"Did you hear him drive off?" the officer
interrupted.

"Come to think of it, I didn't. You suppose

those were Judah-ites? I heard they weren't affected by the sun like we are."

"Don't believe everything you hear, old-timer. I'm going to take a look around. If you help, I'll make sure you get some food."

"Thank you. I've got some stashed away in the freezer. It's not that cold in there since the power's been off. But I wouldn't mind helping you look."

Judd slid back down. "Keep quiet. No movement. Now would be a good time to think of a better hiding place."

"What time does the sun come up here?" Vicki whispered.

"A little after seven, I think," Howard said.

It was 2:15 A.M. when the older man discovered the Beetle hidden below them. Judd moved to the wall and listened as the GC officer searched it. He kicked himself for leaving the guns in the backseat.

"Why would they leave a car out here where it would burn in the morning?" the man said.

"Maybe they're coming back before sunup. You stay with the car. I'll search the garage."

Judd hurried back to Vicki and Howard. "Officer's headed our way."

Howard pointed to a steel ladder that hung over the side of the concrete wall. It was on the opposite side from the Beetle.

"When the guy comes up, we can just hop over and stay until he leaves."

"We'd have to time it so we don't go over until he's reached the top floor," Vicki said.

Judd nodded. "Good. You two stay by the ladder, and I'll crack the door and watch. When I wave, go over and I'll join you."

Vicki and Howard tiptoed to the other side of the roof. Judd propped the door open with a broken piece of concrete and strained to hear any footsteps. His heart beat faster, and he tried to take a deep breath. There was no room for panic now.

Judd couldn't believe the man had seen him in the airport, and he was frustrated they had stayed in the garage. There were a hundred other places in the blocks surrounding the airport that would have made much better hiding places.

Judd glanced at his watch—2:47. Stars shone clear in the sky, and he remembered Ryan Fogarty's favorite bedtime song: *"Twinkle, twinkle, little star, how I wonder what you are. . . ."*

Footsteps on the stairs. Judd moved slightly for a better view and heard a door below open and close. If he was right, the officer was on the third floor, one floor below them. It would take the man five minutes to go through the debris and head for the roof.

At 3:04 a door clattered below him and Judd stood. A flashlight beam darted back and forth on the wall below as the officer trudged up the last flight of stairs. Judd waved wildly at Vicki and Howard and flew across the garage roof to join them. They were over the edge and hanging onto the ladder when Judd scampered over the side. He was just below the top of the wall when the door banged open. Judd sighed and felt something tap his foot.

"Should we go to the third floor?" Howard whispered.

Judd shook his head and mouthed, "Stay here."

Judd listened to the officer and watched for the flashlight beam to come closer.

Suddenly, the man shouted, "He's been up here. I found the empty water bottles and some food wrappers."

"Just one of them or are there more?" the man at the Beetle yelled.

"Can't tell. But the door was propped open. They might still be around somewhere. I'm coming down."

The door hinges creaked as the officer swung it open. Judd smiled. Only four more hours and the sun would be up. A squeal pierced the night, and Judd's heart sank.

His cell phone!

FOURTEEN

Night Moves

JUDD turned off his cell phone and motioned for Vicki and Howard to climb down. The officer rushed toward them above while Judd quickly slid down the ladder and hopped onto the third-floor wall. Vicki and Howard were already running for the stairwell door on the other side of the building.

"They're on the third floor!" the officer yelled, out of breath. "Don't let them get the car!"

Judd raced to catch up as Vicki and Howard ran down the stairs. When Judd hit the door, the officer was still lumbering overhead.

Howard put both hands on the rails and slid down. Vicki took two steps at a time, and Judd caught up to her easily. They were steps away from the second-floor door when the officer burst into the stairwell shouting for them to stop.

"Where now?" Howard called from below.

"Keep going," Judd said. "I don't think the guy outside is armed. And stay close to the wall in case—"

A shot pinged in the stairwell. Vicki screamed, and Judd grabbed her hand as they sprinted down the last flight of stairs. They joined Howard outside and were confronted by the older man holding a metal pole.

"Stop right there!" the man yelled.

Judd pulled Howard to the door. "Jam your foot here and don't let the officer out." Vicki joined him and put her foot against the metal door.

"I'm warning you!" the man said. "Don't come any closer."

Judd had played enough football to know how to make himself look menacing to quarterbacks on the other side of the line. He gritted his teeth and lowered his shoulder. The older man dropped the pole, turned, and ran toward the terminal entrance, just as Judd heard a loud thump at the door behind him.

"What if he shoots?" Vicki said.

"The bullet can't go through—"

Bang!

A one-inch hole appeared in the door and missed Howard by less than a foot.

"Don't make me kill you. Get away from the door!"

Judd picked up the pole and raced forward.

"I'm going to give you one more chance," the officer yelled. "Now stand aside!"

Judd rammed the pole through the door handle and all the way to the other side. He pulled Vicki and Howard away as the officer threw his weight against the door again. It opened a few inches, but no farther.

"Head for the car," Judd hollered, pulling the keys out.

Judd jumped in the driver's side, and the car started with a rumble and clatter. Vicki yelled a warning from the backseat. The officer was aiming at them through metal bars inside the garage. Judd swerved and avoided the first shot. He yelled at Vicki and Howard to get down right before the next shot shattered the back window.

Judd floored the accelerator and pulled away. Unless the officer was a great shot, he'd never hit them, and he didn't. But as they raced out of the airport road, Judd noticed swirling lights.

"We've got a head start, but not much of one," Judd said. "Howard, any ideas on where we should go?"

The VW chugged along as Howard directed Judd through a maze of roads near burned-out buildings. Judd kept his lights off, driving by moonlight and the glow of fires.

"Take a left here," Howard said, and Judd turned into a skate park.

"This is too out in the open," Judd said. "We need to—"

"Go over the curb and down that little hill," Howard said.

"Hang on," Judd said.

They bounced over the curb and raced down an incline, stopping near a drainage pipe twice the size of the car. He pulled in and turned off the motor.

"We used to come down here when one of us was in trouble," Howard said. "You can't see it, but the opening goes all the way to the other side of the road."

"This is perfect," Vicki said.

"Yeah, unless somebody heard us and reports us to the GC," Judd said.

When a vehicle passed overhead, Judd pulled out his phone and turned it on. A call had come from Westin, so Judd dialed him back and explained what had happened. Westin said he had felt guilty for taking off without him. "Where are you now?" Judd said.

"We made it to Kansas before we lost the

sun," Westin said. "Couldn't risk the Wisconsin trip because we were so late. I have some friends here who live close to an old airport. They took us all in. What about Howard?"

Judd gave Westin the good news, and Howard got on the phone and spoke briefly with his mother. He seemed moved by his mom's voice.

"I hope nothing bad happens to these two because of me," Howard said. "All they were trying to do was save me."

Westin told Judd he would fly to the airport with Howard's mother at noon the next day.

"What about the people we were going to take to Wisconsin?" Judd said.

"Change of plans. There's a flight coming from Wyoming in a few hours. These people will go there, while you take Howard and his mom to Wisconsin."

"I have to know, is this going to affect the way the Trib Force looks at me?"

Westin paused. "I told the Trib Force this was my idea."

"But that's not true—"

"Right. So kick me out of the choir. Steele chewed me out, said I was playing hot dog with people's lives, and I apologized."

"But this wasn't your fault. I was the one—"

"Judd, I took the blame. Maybe I shouldn't have, but I did. You're square with them, okay? See you at noon."

Vicki never felt so grateful to see the sun rise the next morning. Instead of being chased like animals, they were free to roam the neighborhoods and head back to the airport.

In a gesture of goodwill, Howard left food in front of the freezer for the old man. "We must have scared him to death last night. Least we can do is give him something to eat."

The flight to Wisconsin went as planned. Howard's mother couldn't stop thanking Judd and Vicki for their help and said she would make it up to them somehow.

The group in Wisconsin welcomed the two newcomers with open arms. Howard seemed most pleased to meet Zeke, who looked nothing like what he expected in an "assistant pastor."

The Tribulation Force continued moving people and supplies around the country and the world, though the Global Community had tried to adapt. News from Oregon disturbed Vicki and the others when they found out about a new GC plan that affected believers.

"The GC moved into the lava tubes in Oregon," Mark said a few days after Judd and Vicki returned.

"Lava tubes?" Charlie said.

"They're natural rock formations made by volcanoes," Mark said. "Miles of tunnels believers have been using since we were forced to go underground. Once the plague of heat hit, GC survivors decided to move into them at night because the temperature is so cool during the day. They surprised some believers, and a bunch of them were executed."

"Why couldn't someone have helped?" Vicki said.

"These believers were pretty cut off from anyone outside. They were living on their own."

Other members of the Tribulation Force passed along stories of believers eluding the GC in China, the Philippines, Australia, and other locations. The 144,000 evangelists continued their preaching, and many undecided became believers. This encouraged the Wisconsin group, knowing that there were still some without Carpathia's mark, but everyone knew the numbers were dwindling.

Though Vicki didn't like to be separated from Judd, they each took separate trips as requested by the Tribulation Force to help believers with supplies, food, and new places to live. In some cases, Vicki was asked to go because she had been the main contact for younger believers who had seen her at one of the stadium events. At other locations, the Trib Force needed help loading and unloading materials, and Judd volunteered. Most of these were daylong flights or drives, so they were back with each other the next day.

As time went on, Vicki wondered what Judd was thinking about their relationship. They had become more serious, and everyone in the Wisconsin group wondered if Judd would propose. "I'm content however things work out," Vicki told her friends, "but I'll admit I wouldn't mind being Mrs. Judd Thompson."

Judd agonized over the marriage question. He knew Vicki was the one for him, if he did decide to get married, but things seemed to be going so well that he didn't want to mess up their friendship. Judd pored over the Scriptures and asked people's advice.

Zeke was a big help, saying that if God planted a desire for marriage, there wasn't anything to hold him back. "You have to ask yourself—are you ready to love another human being the way God loves you?"

On a trip to Tennessee to help out a group
that had befriended him, Judd opened the
Bible to the passage in 1 Corinthians, chapter
13. Known as the love chapter, Judd read the
verses, then wrote a segment of the passage
in his own words.

> *Love is so patient and kind that others
> can see it, taste it, and smell it. Love isn't
> jealous when someone else succeeds, isn't
> rude, doesn't boast, and certainly isn't
> prideful. Love doesn't want things a certain
> way and doesn't get irritated over little
> things. Love doesn't keep a scorecard. When
> a wrong is committed, a person who loves
> doesn't hold that over the other person's
> head. A person who loves isn't glad about
> people who are treated unfairly, but is glad
> when the truth is seen and welcomed. Love
> simply does not give up, it never loses faith
> or hope, and in every circumstance, no
> matter what that circumstance is, love keeps
> on going.*

Judd studied the list and shook his head.
Love is pretty tough to accomplish, he thought.
As he looked over his words and the other
parts of the passage, he was struck by how
many of these verses Vicki lived. She was
never jealous of anyone who succeeded, was

never proud or boastful about her accomplishments, and seemed to always put others ahead of herself. Even when Judd was asked to go on trips for the Trib Force, she seemed genuinely excited for his opportunities.

Though it scared him, it was on that flight that Judd finally made up his mind to ask Vicki the most important question of his life. *"Perfect love expels all fear,"* Judd thought. Zeke loved quoting that verse. Maybe he was right.

Vicki was excited when Judd asked her to help him deliver supplies to a Wisconsin group she had never heard of. Judd said they would be gone a few hours and that she might want to bring some food along, so she packed a lunch and they set out after ten that morning.

They chatted about the way things were going with the group, how much help Charlie had been, and how glad they were that he had become part of the group. Vicki had received an e-mail from Wanda that morning reporting good progress by Cheryl.

"You think she'll ever come back?" Judd said.

"Wanda doesn't think it's a good idea yet,

but if Cheryl keeps working on getting healthy—" Vicki pointed to her head—"I wouldn't be surprised to see her again."

"Ryan Victor sure is full of spunk," Judd said.

Vicki laughed and repeated a story about the boy Josey had told her the day before. Ryan had truly been the bright spot in their lives the past two years.

Vicki noticed a cloud of dust in one of the mirrors and turned. "Do you see that?"

Judd glanced back. "Looks like smoke from a building."

"No, it came from beside the road, like someone just pulled out." Vicki peered through the back windshield and yelped. "Judd, there's a car coming this way."

"Well, we don't have anything to worry about, right? It has to be a believer or the car would be burning up by now."

"I suppose you're right, but what if the plague's lifted? Or maybe the GC has figured out a way to overcome the effects—"

"I see lights on top of that car," Judd interrupted.

"Step on it. We can lose whoever it is in this Humvee."

Judd sped up, but the car gained on them. Vicki's heart beat faster and faster.

The car was right behind them and Judd slowed.

"What are you doing? Keep going."

"Let's see who it is."

"What are you talking about? That guy's GC. I know it!"

Judd pulled to the side of the road and stopped. Vicki stared in disbelief as a man in a Global Community uniform stepped from the car pointing a gun at the Humvee.

Judd rolled down his window and studied the rearview mirror. "Let's play this straight. Just do what he says and we'll be okay."

"Both of you step out of the car," the officer said.

Judd put a hand on Vicki's shoulder. "We'll be okay. Just get out."

Vicki opened the door and climbed out. She looked for a place to run, but the officer motioned her to the rear of the Humvee. The air felt warm, so the plague was still in effect.

"You, redhead, walk slowly toward me with your hands up," the officer said.

Vicki did as she was told.

"What do you want with us?" Judd said.

"Shut up and come with me, punk."

"No!" Vicki said.

"Hands on the back of the car!" the officer warned.

Vicki turned. She couldn't believe they had

been caught. They had gone through so much, too much to have it end like this.

"You," the officer said to Judd, "on your knees."

Judd knelt behind the car, and Vicki glanced at the officer, who slowly walked toward them. The man stopped near Judd, holstered his gun, and pulled something out of his pocket. "I believe this is yours, young man. And I think you know what to do with it."

Vicki turned, her brow furrowed. The officer had given Judd a tiny box, and Judd smiled. The officer took off his sunglasses and pushed his hat up, showing the mark of the true believer.

"Zeke?" Vicki said.

"Pay attention to what's happening, redhead," Zeke said.

Vicki glanced at Judd, who was still on one knee. "Vicki, I have known you almost six years, and though we've had some difficult days, the last few weeks have been the happiest of my life."

Vicki covered her mouth with a hand as Judd opened the box, revealing a sparkling ring.

"I've come to love you, Vicki, and I want to share the rest of my days with you, before our Lord returns." He pulled the ring from the box and held it out. His voice broke when he said, "Will you marry me?"

Tears stung Vicki's eyes as she slipped the ring on her finger. Vicki fell into Judd's arms and they kissed. Her voice trembled as she whispered, "Yes."

FIFTEEN

Westin's Idea

WHEN Vicki returned to the camp in Avery, the others had put together an engagement party for her and Judd. Zeke had told everyone what was going on, and Josey had made a cake.

Lionel could hardly contain himself. He kept slapping Judd on the back, smiling, laughing, and shaking his head. "You finally did it!"

After Vicki recovered from the shock of the creative way Judd had asked her to marry him, she socked him in the shoulder for scaring her with the GC trick. "You just about gave me a heart attack! I thought we were both dead."

Judd smiled. "I thought it would be memorable. Who wants to tell everybody a boring engagement story?"

They both met with Marshall to talk about their next step. To her surprise, Vicki discovered there were a few at the camp who thought it wasn't a good idea for them to get married.

"I've had conversations with some who think these kinds of things shouldn't be happening," Marshall said. "But this is a personal decision, and you two have shown good judgment through this dating process."

"What do you mean?" Judd said.

"Let's just say people have been watching you two to see if you'd become clingy with each other. You know, to see if you'd be so 'in love' that you wouldn't be able to concentrate on anything else. But we've been pleased with how you've handled this."

"Vicki and I were talking about dates for the wedding," Judd said. "Is there a set waiting period?"

"That's up to you, though I would suggest you go through a marriage counseling course."

"What will that do?" Vicki said.

"It helps prepare you for the big changes ahead. We could set up the sessions and have them done as fast as possible."

Judd bit his lip. "I know this is a long shot, but would there be any way to link with Dr. Ben-Judah and have him perform the ceremony?"

"We were talking," Vicki continued, "and outside of Bruce Barnes, the person who has mentored us most is Dr. Ben-Judah, even though it's been mostly through his writing."

Marshall scratched his chin. "Why don't you e-mail him and see?"

Judd wrote the e-mail and let Vicki read it. "Perfect," she said. He sent it directly to Dr. Ben-Judah and copied Sam Goldberg and Mr. Stein. Vicki wrote Chloe Steele and a few others she thought would be interested in their news. Within an hour, a flood of messages came back.

I'm so happy for you, Vicki and Judd, Chloe wrote. *I think you'll find marriage one of the most challenging and rewarding things you'll ever do. I can't imagine not having married Buck, in spite of how little time we have left.*

Rayford Steele also wrote. Judd was a little anxious, but he was relieved when he read Rayford's message. *I've been married twice, and only once as a believer. Having someone share the good and bad times is one of the greatest comforts I've experienced. You two will be a great team!*

Westin wrote from his plane somewhere

over the Atlantic Ocean. *I couldn't be happier for you. Actually, I might be able to give you a pretty good present. Let me know when you two are planning the ceremony.*

"What could he be talking about?" Vicki said.

Judd shrugged. "Knowing Westin, it could be anything."

The next day Dr. Ben-Judah wrote and congratulated Judd and Vicki. *I would be proud to unite the two of you if we can work out the technical details. In the meantime, you should both seek the Lord in prayer as to where you should live. It may be that he wants you to stay in Wisconsin with your friends. We could also use a young married couple here in Petra. Consider this and let me know when you would like to arrange the ceremony.*

Vicki's mouth opened wide. "I've heard so much about Petra, but I can't imagine actually living there."

"It would be a great place to start a new life," Judd said. "But what about our friends?"

"It'd be hard to leave, but if we're together, I could call anywhere home."

Two weeks later, just after a counseling

session with Marshall, Mark held up the phone in the main cabin. "It's Westin. I think you'll want to take this."

Judd heard plane noise as he answered the phone. "New plan," Westin said. "And you should know I've cleared this with the Trib Force."

"What are you talking about?"

"Remember my surprise to you and Vicki? Well, I heard about Dr. Ben-Judah's offer to have you come to Petra. I have an important run next week to some believers near New Babylon, and I'd like you to come with me."

"Just me?" Judd said.

"Last trip as a bachelor," Westin said. "You help me with the New Babylon drop, and then we go to Petra so you can build your honeymoon cottage."

"I've seen the homes there, and there's not much to them."

"Still, you could get things ready for Vicki. Then she'd come on my next trip back."

Judd looked at Vicki and smiled. "What about my best man? He's here in Wisconsin."

"I can bring him with Vicki and anybody else who might want to relocate to the safest place on earth."

Vicki hugged Judd tightly and looked into his eyes. "The next time I see you, I'll be walking down the aisle—or the rocks or whatever they call it in Petra."

"I don't think I can find a tux," Judd said, "I hope you won't be too disappointed."

"Something about this plan scares me," Vicki said.

"We've waited this long. Another week's not a big deal."

"Just be careful."

Judd met Westin in Hudson, Wisconsin, and was amazed at the amount of supplies packed onto the plane. Westin said the believers near New Babylon were a little mysterious, not having much contact with the outside world, but they were prepared to ride out their remaining days right under the noses of the Global Community. The contact they had made with Westin wasn't through the Tribulation Force but from a man named Otto, who had moved to New Babylon from Germany.

"That's about all I know," Westin said, "other than they've been fighting the GC every chance they get."

"You mean fighting, as in guns?" Judd said.

"Hey, the last battle is coming, and you need to get ready. Armageddon. I'm not going to miss it."

"I thought Armageddon was where God smashed the armies of the Antichrist."

"It is, but God's used his followers up to now, so why wouldn't he use us in battle? You should hear Dr. Ben-Judah preach about it. He's really stirred me up to think I can be part of it."

Judd settled in for the long flight and sent Vicki an e-mail. *When the disappearances happened, it was scary and really sad. But part of it was exciting because we were on our own, without parents telling us what to do. But like Marshall told us in one of our sessions, everything we do from now on will be done together!*

The plane touched down near Petra, and Judd spent a day meeting old friends and scouting a place to build a small shelter. Sam Goldberg showed him several sites, and Mr. Stein said there would be plenty of help and materials.

"We don't have all the modern conveniences," Mr. Stein said, "but we have fresh food provided by God every day and wonderful teaching, not to mention fresh water."

After visiting the communications center and greeting Naomi Tiberius, Judd rested for the trip the next day to New Babylon.

Vicki watched the news coverage about changes in the past two days and felt concerned about Judd. The blood had turned back to water in streams, signaling the end of the third Bowl Judgment. An urgent message from Chang Wong came not long after.

> *In my monitoring of Carpathia over the last few days, I believe we have reached a turning point. He is still occupied with the "Jewish problem," as he calls it. Just when Carpathia and Akbar thought they had devised a plan to kill Jewish believers in Jerusalem, the sun plague hit and the GC were sent underground. In fact, the number of Global Community forces who have died is staggering. But they still have a lot of firepower available.*
>
> *Of particular interest to me was a phone call I recorded between the potentate and his security chief, Suhail Akbar. I send this transcript not to scare but to warn you of the seriousness of the threat.*

Carpathia: Suhail, these plagues have always had their seasons. This one has to end sometime. And when it does, that may be the time for us to pull out the half of our munitions and equipment that we have in reserve. Would you estimate that the confidentiality level on that stockpile remains secure?

Akbar: To the best of my knowledge, Excellency.

Carpathia: When the sun curse lifts, Director, when you can stand being out in the light of day again, let us be ready to mount the most massive offensive in the history of mankind. I have not yet conceded even Petra, but I want the Jews wherever they are. I want them from Israel, particularly Jerusalem. And I will not be distracted or dissuaded by our whining friends in northern Africa. Suhail, if you have ever wanted to please me, ever wanted to impress me, ever wanted to make yourself indispensable to me, give yourself to this task. The planning, the strategy, the use of resources should make every other war strate-

gist in history hang his head in
shame. I want you to knock me out,
Suhail, and I am telling you that
resources—monetary and military—
are limitless.

Akbar: Thank you, sir. I won't let
you down.

Carpathia: Did you get that,
Suhail? Lim-it-less.

After Judd's plane touched down in a remote
area outside of New Babylon, he met with
one of the leaders of the mysterious group,
Rainer Kurtzmann, a former stage actor from
Germany who had become a believer not
long after the disappearances.

After Judd and the others loaded supplies
into several of the group's vehicles and headed
for Carpathia's city, Rainer took another route
to give Judd and Westin a tour. The effects of
the sun plague had left the city in ruins. Lavish
parks with fountains and flowers were
reduced to ashes. Judd noticed Rainer was
wearing a gun, and Judd asked him why.

"We came from Germany, where fighting
the GC was getting boring. One of the leaders of a nearby group, Otto Weser, convinced
us from Scripture that there would be believ-

ers in New Babylon during this time. So we came, and we have survived."

"I can't imagine living here without the mark of Carpathia, right under his nose," Judd said.

"I couldn't either. Some said we would be killed before we ever found a place to stay, but here we are, moving supplies into our underground hideout."

"Have you lost any members?"

Rainer gave Judd a pained look. "Yes, but I'd rather not talk about that now."

Judd nodded.

Back at the safe house, Judd and the others enjoyed a meal together. Everyone wanted to hear about Judd's experience in New Babylon, and he described his adventures, though he kept the information about Chang Wong private.

The conversation was so interesting that Judd and Westin stayed past their deadline to get back to Petra before dark, so the group made room for them. As the sun went down, Judd watched the group go through their complex routine of securing the hideout. A few days after the sun plague began, the group had burned the top of their house to make it look like the others surrounding it.

Judd found it difficult to sleep in the

enclosed hideaway. It was so different than the camp in Wisconsin, where they felt safe at all hours. A team kept watch over video screens throughout the night, looking for any irregular GC movement.

When morning came, Judd headed outside to watch the sunrise but was stopped by a female member of the group. "We aren't allowed out until the sun is fully up. I'm sorry."

Judd went to the breakfast area, where he wouldn't disturb anyone, and dialed Chang Wong.

Chang was out of breath when he answered the private line. "Judd, I hope you're calling from Petra."

"Actually, I'm not. Why?"

"Show's over."

"What?"

"Though I've been immune to the sun plague, I've still felt the difference in temperature and humidity. A few minutes ago I woke up, and the air feels different." Judd heard Chang clicking at his computer. "Yeah, I'm right. The temperature here is normal."

Judd's heart sank. "Maybe when the sun gets higher—"

"No, usually at this time of the morning things have begun to burn."

Judd tried to hold back his emotion. He

had tried so hard to get back to Vicki, and now he was a million miles from her in the most hostile location on the planet.

"Where are you?" Chang said.

"You're not going to believe it," Judd said.

ABOUT THE AUTHORS

Jerry B. Jenkins (www.jerryjenkins.com) is the writer of the Left Behind series. He owns the Jerry B. Jenkins Christian Writers Guild, an organization dedicated to mentoring aspiring authors. Former vice president for publishing for the Moody Bible Institute of Chicago, he also served many years as editor of *Moody* magazine and is now Moody's writer-at-large.

His writing has appeared in publications as varied as *Reader's Digest, Parade, Guideposts,* in-flight magazines, and dozens of other periodicals. Jenkins's biographies include books with Billy Graham, Hank Aaron, Bill Gaither, Luis Palau, Walter Payton, Orel Hershiser, and Nolan Ryan, among many others. His books appear regularly on the *New York Times, USA Today, Wall Street Journal,* and *Publishers Weekly* best-seller lists.

Jerry is also the writer of the nationally syndicated sports story comic strip *Gil Thorp,* distributed to newspapers across the United States by Tribune Media Services.

Jerry and his wife, Dianna, live in Colorado and have three grown sons.

Dr. Tim LaHaye (www.timlahaye.com), who conceived the idea of fictionalizing an account of the Rapture and the Tribulation, is a noted author, minister, and nationally recognized speaker on Bible prophecy. He is the founder of both Tim LaHaye Ministries and The PreTrib Research Center. He also recently cofounded the Tim LaHaye School of Prophecy at Liberty University. Presently Dr. LaHaye speaks at many of the major Bible prophecy conferences in the U.S. and Canada, where his current prophecy books are very popular.

Dr. LaHaye holds a doctor of ministry degree from Western Theological Seminary and a doctor of literature degree from Liberty University. For twenty-five years he pastored one of the nation's outstanding churches in San Diego, which grew to three locations. It was during that time that he founded two accredited Christian high schools, a Christian school system of ten schools, and Christian Heritage College.

Dr. LaHaye has written over forty books that have been published in more than thirty languages. He has written books on a wide variety of subjects, such as family life, temperaments, and Bible prophecy. His current fiction works, the Left Behind series, written with Jerry B. Jenkins, continue to appear on the best-seller lists of the Christian Booksellers Association, *Publishers Weekly, Wall Street Journal, USA Today,* and the *New York Times.*

He is the father of four grown children and grandfather of nine. Snow skiing, waterskiing, motorcycling, golfing, vacationing with family, and jogging are among his leisure activities.

The Future Is Clear

Check out the exciting Left Behind: The Kids series

BOOKS #39 AND #40 COMING SOON!

Discover the latest about the Left Behind series and complete line of products at

www.leftbehind.com

Hooked on the exciting
Left Behind: The Kids series?
Then you'll love the dramatic audios!

Listen as the characters come to life in this theatrical
audio that makes the saga of those left behind
even more exciting.

High-tech sound effects, original music,
and professional actors will have you
on the edge of your seat.

Experience the heart-stopping action and suspense of the end times for yourself!

Five exciting volumes available on CD or cassette.